FRIENDS
OF ACPL

Storm over the Blue Hills

Storm over the

Blue Hills

ALAN C. JENKINS

Illustrated by
VICTOR AMBRUS

W · W · NORTON & COMPANY · INC · *New York*

Author's Note

WHEN I was in India, I became deeply interested in the Todas, a tribe living in the Nilgiris or "Blue Hills" of western Madras State. I visited these people in their homes, enjoyed their hospitality, watched their various festivals and saw the magnificent buffalo for which they are renowned and on which they depend in every way. Alas, ironical though it is in face of India's ever-increasing millions, the Todas are a vanishing people, being numbered today in hundreds. Their origin is uncertain, one legend about them being that they are descended from the remnants of Alexander the Great's army, a colourful but unlikely theory. This story is based on the Toda way of life, and the customs and beliefs I have described—even the names I have used—are fully authentic. At the same time this book is not to be taken as an absolutely detailed account either of the Todas themselves or of the Nilgiris where they live.

A. C. J.

To Karl Nickul

Contents

1	The Death Chase	9
2	The Invisible Door	16
3	Honour to the House	23
4	The Buffalo Bell	31
5	For Moon Horn's Sake	41
6	Land of Strangers	52
7	The God in the River	62
8	The Bread of Companionship	71
9	The Royal Hunt	80
10	Fear in the Night	87
11	God's Flower	94
12	The Worst Torture of All	106
13	The Bullocks Tread the Grain	116
14	The Pattern is Woven	124
15	The Thread is Broken	132
16	Storm over the Blue Hills	142
17	Accuser and Accused	151
18	The Storm Passes	157

1 *The Death Chase*

KISHKAR drew his embroidered robe closely about him, and muffled his grave, dark face in a fold of it. The air was sharp in the glades and hollows where the sun had not yet reached. Patches of hoar frost powdered the base of the gorse bushes which spotted the wild, rolling downland of the Blue Hills.

He listened to the scutter of hooves from lower down the grassy slopes, the screams and shouts of mingled dismay and exultation. He watched the black king vulture wheeling tirelessly overhead, its superbly insolent flight a series of faultless convolutions and arabesques. It was strange that something so beautiful on the wing should be such a waddling scavenger when it descended to earth.

The vulture knew that death was imminent. So did Moon Horn, the buffalo heifer, who grazed a sunset shadow's length away. Kishkar glanced round almost guiltily as the little buffalo raised her damp muzzle and sniffed the air, as if recognizing the taint of blood even before it had been spilt.

Kishkar too knew that death was close, and if it had not been for Moon Horn he would have gloried in the fact. For it was the custom and he would have wished to take part in the death chase down there, where the older youths pursued the buffalo that must die in order to lead the woman Sindavul into the world of the dead.

None but the buffaloes could conduct the dead safely into the shades. It had always been so, ever since the People of the Buffalo had lived in the Blue Hills. The great god Ouen had decreed it long ages ago, when he first awoke and created the People. Therefore it must be right.

Kishkar himself had never questioned the custom. You might just as well doubt whether it was right for the sun to rise every morning or for the monsoon rain to fall on the parched earth at the appointed time. Equally, it was quite natural that whenever anyone died, like Sindavul now, one of the buffaloes should be led to the death stone and slain.

It was only occasionally that Kishkar thought with dread of the possibility that Moon Horn herself might have to be sacrificed. What if Kwodron, his father, died? Or his mother, Moutouvelli . . . or his sister, Laxam . . . or even Tipane, his young brother, who was scampering down there unlawfully on the fringe of the death chase? Wouldn't the best buffalo among his father's herd have to be killed?

Kwodron possessed some fine beasts, powerful bulls, cows that had borne many fine calves. But Moon Horn had a twisted tail, sure sign of her divine pedigree. It was a mark that appeared from time to time among the buffaloes of the Blue Hills and it came about thus.

When the great god Ouen awoke from his sleep, he plunged an iron bar into the hillside, and into the hole he made he thrust his arm and drew out many fine buffaloes. Clinging to the tail of the last buffalo was the first man. It was thus that certain buffaloes still had a twisted tail, to remind the People of the Buffalo of their humble origin. Such a buffalo was immensely valuable: no dead person need fear losing the way to the shades if he were conducted by a buffalo such as that.

Kishkar drew his white robe, with its red, blue and black edging, more tightly round him. Now it was not the frost that sent a tremor through his slim body. He could not bear to think of Moon Horn being sacrificed.

The buffalo heifer was of great consequence in Kishkar's life. Indeed, though he did not think of it like that, the heifer symbolized his way of life, the life of the People of the Buffalo. He had looked after Moon Horn since she was a tiny calf, and he was the only person who could handle her, for the buffalo of the Blue Hills were renowned for their fierceness—the cows were sometimes even fiercer than the bulls. The animals roamed half wild across the undulating downs, kept for the rich milk the cows gave and for the sacred purpose of leading the dead safely into the next world. Kishkar's people never touched their meat. It was only unworthy people such as the Kothas and the Badagas who ate flesh.

Kishkar's breath came more urgently as he turned to watch Moon Horn cropping the abundant grass, crisply, intently. She was magnificent, with her profound, moist brown eyes, with their hint of smoky blue, and the corded muscles rippling under her sleek brown hide. In her supple carriage and clean limbs strength and grace mingled. But above all, her crowning glory was the tall, curving horns, fluent as a poem, the tips curving towards each other as exact as a rhyme.

Kishkar glowed with delight as he surveyed her. It was he who had given Moon Horn her name, a secret name nobody else knew—not even Sadamut with whom he shared most things, though not so much now that she was beginning to waste time twisting her hair into ringlets and larding them with rancid butter as if she were a grown woman.

He had called the buffalo Moon Horn because, one evening when he was with the herdsmen, he had seen her drinking in a pool where the trembling reflection of the moon was caught in the reflection of the buffalo's horns. It had seemed so splendid that Kishkar had composed the name there and then.

But all at once, as if to shatter these proud thoughts, the clamour of the death chase burst out more violently below him. They were coming nearer. There was triumph now in the wild voices. He forgot Moon Horn and ran a little way down the slope to see better, for he guessed the chase was moving through the grove of blue-gum trees in one of the glades that cleft the hills.

Hooves thundered over the resilient turf, desperate, weary. Voices shrilled upon the air like those of flocks of ugly birds gathering round carrion. It was strange—though it did not seem so to Kishkar—that the People of the Buffalo, who never knew the taste of meat, should exult at the prospect of bloodshed. But only the blood of the buffalo could open the way to paradise!

Tensely, expectantly, Kishkar came to a halt at the crest of the slope. Immediately below him, so close he could have dropped a stone on it, a buffalo came into view. Its flanks heaved, its mouth slavered. He could hear the panting gusts of breath above the shambling of its hooves. Behind it, drawing ever closer on both sides, raced the young men of the People of the Buffalo, their white garments splashing against the green of the turf and the speckled gold of the gorse flowers. In the wake of them all Tipane still stumbled breathlessly, determined to keep up. He would get into trouble if Kwodron knew he was there where he had no right.

The strident shouts dinned in Kishkar's ears and he

clenched his fists and wanted to shout too. One day, when he had passed the test, he would take part in the death chase. He would be the one to capture the sacrificial buffalo, lead it to the death stone. Now he watched as, barefoot, some of them almost naked, for they had thrown off their few clothes, the young men raced eagerly after the tiring buffalo. If it had the sense to run straight, make off into the vastness of the Blue Hills, it might escape. But in panic, well knowing that death was at hand, it jinked and swerved here and there, changed its mind with every shambling stride, then blundered on again.

The chase passed on and away through the gorse bushes and the lantana scrub and Kishkar went running headlong down the slope for fear of being left behind.

Breathless, scratched by thorns, sometimes thrown violently on his elbows by the steepness of the grassy slope, he hurried on. A startled jackal loped away from under a bush and eyed him with a gasping, apprehensive look, but Kishkar took no notice of it.

When he ran out into the glade the buffalo had turned at bay. One of the young men drew ahead of his companions, closed in swiftly towards it and leapt at it. But the buffalo turned and laboured on—with a savage thrust of its curving horns it flung him off on to the ground, where he sprawled while the rest trampled past him. Their surging shouts drowned his groans.

Now a second youth, Kishkar's cousin Punog, had darted in at the weary buffalo. He was more successful. He seized the animal by the horns and, though he was dragged along bodily, did not let go. His head bobbed up and down like that of a swimmer fighting the waves and Kishkar thought the buffalo would get the best of that fearful struggle.

But the buffalo was already exhausted from the long, bewildering chase. Its once fierce strength had ebbed and it could not resist the will of a determined man. The running fight turned into a mad scuffle, but at length the buffalo gave in abruptly. With drooping head it stood submissively, snorting and panting as if its lungs were torn.

Punog straightened his naked back, pressed against the shoulder of the animal. Chest labouring, limbs glossy with sweat, he surveyed his companions triumphantly as they hurried towards him.

Meanwhile, more spectators had come thronging up through the blue-gum glades to partake of the young men's triumph, older men who had done all this before, and small, excited boys, to whom Tipane boasted shrilly of how he had helped in the death chase. In a jostling, incoherent company they marched with the captured buffalo, which the young men led firmly by the horns.

On the fringe of the crowd Kishkar hurried, savouring at second hand all the thrills and dangers of the ceremony that had just finished, and even more the mysterious, inexpressible exultation that all the People of the Buffalo felt in the awareness of the doomed animal's sacred mission.

Down past banks of saucer-big daisies and burnished gorse the crowd went pattering, on towards the death stone, round which the Kotha drums and pipes played a welcome. Elated, shouting his praise of Punog, Kishkar pressed on with the rest, eager to feel part of the triumph that had been achieved. Tipane pushed his way through to his brother's side, abashed now that his father might question where he had been.

As the crowd filed down towards the grove of bluegums where many more of the People of the Buffalo waited, Kishkar looked back at the rolling crest of the downland hills that had begun to shimmer now as the tropical sun beat out its silent, brassy gong.

Silhouetted on the distant skyline stood Moon Horn. The buffalo heifer had paused in her grazing and, with her splendid head raised questioningly, seemed to be looking down at the crowd.

Kishkar felt a catch at his heart. The shout of triumph faded on his lips. His mouth was full of dust as he stumbled on in the wake of the people. Tipane was crying out something, but he took no notice. The sound of the drums was like the sound of doom.

2 The Invisible Door

THE music of the Kothas grew louder. The hand-slap of
the shallow little drums became as insistent as a nagging
thought. The shrill notes of the pipes insinuated themselves
on the air. The Kothas shuffled and bobbed, playing their
best in order to ingratiate themselves with the People of
the Buffalo.

It was always the Kothas who provided the music. Long
ago, when the People were Lords of the Hills, the Kothas
were in thrall to them. Now, they were free, but they
continued to do service in certain ways. In addition to
their music, they brought fruit and grains to their one-time
masters in return for the carcases of the sacrificial buffaloes.

Kishkar and Tipane were caught up willy-nilly in the
procession that led the buffalo down towards the death
stone. The wretched animal was almost hidden by the
crowd of men all eager to claim that they had taken part
in the affair. Even that stupid Kushken had managed to
get his hand on a horn, pretending he had had something
to do with it, though he was only a few months older than
Kishkar. Kushken caught Kishkar's eye and raised his
chin arrogantly and shouted more stridently than ever to
hide his foolishness. Tipane turned to yell an insult at
him, but Kishkar dragged his brother away.

The dust churned up by many naked feet glinted in the
sunlight. The jostling of many bodies, the panting of

16

breath, the babble of voices, created a blanket of sound. But now the triumphant shouting diminished, for the people were aware of the solemnity of the occasion. The drum-slaps beat out their doomful phrase. The pipes uttered their wailing threnody. Kishkar's dark brown eyes were heavy with awe as he pressed on with the throng. He found difficulty in breathing. The thumping of his heart echoed the muffled slapping of the little drums.

Near the death stone another group of people waited, men of stately carriage. They were handsome of feature, with long thick sculpted hair and patriarchal beards. Their voluminous robes trailed on the ground. Kwodron was among them and the boys broke away from the crowd and ran towards their father. Kishkar flung himself on his knees in front of the man and, taking each of Kwodron's feet in turn between his hands, placed it briefly on his forehead in token of respect. Kwodron smiled gravely and nodded in approval at his son. Tipane bumped the earth with his head in his eagerness to follow Kishkar.

As the procession reached the death stone, Paramajoti the dairy-priest stepped forward, slowly, majestically, conscious of his dignity and importance. At once the crowd grew silent, for Paramajoti was highest among the People of the Buffalo. He alone might handle the milk on which they depended for their sustenance. He alone might enter the dairy-temple and distribute the milk to the women who came at appointed times with their brass chattis. Above all, only Paramajoti might handle the sacred Buffalo Bell, talisman of the People, which hung, unseen by any other eyes, in the temple.

Kishkar's mouth was dry as he regarded Paramajoti. He had to put a hand to his lips to stifle a cry of joy, for suddenly he thought again of the incredible fact that he,

Kishkar, son of Kwodron, might be appointed the dairy-priest's acolyte. It had all come about by chance, this dazzling possibility, when Tormungudur, the boy appointed to the office two years ago, died. Now another must take his place.

It was known that Paramajoti looked with favour upon Kwodron's family. True, Kishkar was nearly fourteen and the custom was that a boy of twelve years should be appointed. But at present there was no boy of the right age and character among the People of the Buffalo, who were so few in numbers. It was rumoured that soon Kishkar would indeed be chosen and receive the special branding on his right shoulder, which was to help him milk skilfully without getting tired. Kishkar glowed with excitement at these thoughts. His eyes dilated proudly. One day he might even take Paramajoti's place, as the most revered man among the People.

At his side somebody shouldered him roughly. A foot stepped on his own naked foot and he cried out in protest. It was Kushken who had come shoving past him to get a better view. It was as if Kushken had jealously read Kishkar's thoughts, for he too hoped that he might be chosen to take Tormungudur's place.

"Make way for one who has taken part in the death chase," said Kushken.

"As well might the jackal pretend to have driven the sambar into the tiger's jaws," screeched Tipane, using an elbow to hold back the brash Kushken, though he was ready to dart behind his brother for protection. "You did not appear until we had the buffalo safely in our grasp." He glanced furtively at Kishkar to see his reaction at this boasting.

But Kishkar, ignoring Kushken, sternly whispered to

Tipane to behave, for Paramajoti had begun to bless the buffalo, which the young men held firmly in front of him. Its eyes rolled, its neck strained, its hooves dug into the turf. Apparently the buffalo did not appreciate the sacred mission for which it was being made ready. In the name of the sun and the moon and all the mysteries and wonders of nature, Paramajoti the dairy-priest dedicated the buffalo. While he spoke, dropping each word as if he were doling out precious coins, people came forward with flowers in tribute to the animal.

Brilliant flame-of-the-forest petals, purple wreath-flowers, luminous white moonbeam flowers, all these and many others were garlanded upon the buffalo, a soft, fluttering mosaic of colour sprinkled about its neck and muzzle. Always near, the music of the Kothas kept up its monotonous refrain.

Now the people stirred restlessly, for Kunparadi had walked to the priest's side, bearing the stone sledge-hammer on his shoulder. Kunparadi was the strongest man even among the men of the Blue Hills. He was an imposing figure, with his silky beard and proud face and tall frame that moved so athletically under his long robe.

Kishkar trembled. Even Tipane was glad to put a hand in his brother's. The crowd murmured in anticipation, brown faces grave. The moment of sacrifice had come, the moment when that mysterious, invisible door of death would open and the sacred buffalo would lead the spirit of Sindavul into eternity, there to await the coming of all other men and women who would follow in the fullness of time.

Now Kunparadi had removed his robe. Utter silence fell upon the glade except for the stertorous breathing of the crowd and the uneasy shuffle of bodies unable to endure

19

the tension. Somewhere a tiny verditer flycatcher set up its tinkling cry and the sound was loud as a solemn bell in the foreboding stillness.

Kishkar swayed as he watched Kunparadi raise his sledge-hammer. Suddenly the image of Moon Horn had come before him. For one terrible moment he thought of Moon Horn standing submissively there, held on either side by the escort of strong young men whose bodies gleamed with sweat.

Kishkar tried to cry out to stop Kunparadi. He tried to rush forward to save Moon Horn, but neither his voice nor his body would act. A fearful dumbness possessed him: his limbs seemed turned to water. Helplessly he watched while the heavy sledge-hammer came up in a slow, deliberate arc.

Then, driven by the powerful muscles of Kunparadi, the great hammer descended, stooping more swiftly than a falcon at its prey. A vehement crack rang out through the glade, as if a tree had been felled by a lightning-shaft.

The crowd sighed in awe and ecstasy. The pole-axed buffalo tottered. The young men had stepped aside. The animal stretched out its wet muzzle, its eyes glazed over like the sun obscured by a cloud. Then it slumped down, lifeless, on the turf, while the flower petals were wafted round it.

It had all been quick, merciful. Kunparadi was strong, his eye sure. Already the spirit of the buffalo had departed on its mission. Already other grinning, turbanned Kothas were waiting in the background with their ropes and bullocks to haul away the useless carcase.

Where had the buffalo spirit gone? Why could you never see it? Staring at the stricken animal stretched out there, Kishkar wondered this as he always did. Where did the buffaloes lead the dead? To a country that resembled the Blue Hills? It would be exciting to see that country, speak again to the people who went there. If he could go there accompanied by Moon Horn he would not be afraid. But until he could be sure of that he was glad it was not Moon Horn but another buffalo which had been sacrificed.

All at once he was aware of somebody tugging urgently at him.

"You are hurting my hand," Tipane complained. "You're holding it so tight."

Kishkar stared in astonishment at his brother and let go.

Now the boys found themselves swept forward by the crowd again, for Sindavul's bier was approaching through the glade, between the slender blue-gums, past the coconut-scented gorse bushes, whose flowers looked like tiny shards of the sun. Above the tireless repetition of the drums and the long pipes rose the sound of wailing. Many in the crowd added their groans of sympathy.

Clad in her best embroidered robe and bedecked with all her rings and necklaces and shell ornaments, Sindavul was borne on a bier of bamboo poles carried on the shoulders of half a dozen men. Behind her shuffled the mourners in clothes that dripped a trail of water, for all had bathed ritually before the funeral. Wailing in many keys, shouting dementedly, tearing their garments, they followed the bier towards the funeral pyre, the men in front, the musicians behind them, the womenfolk bringing up the rear. The hills echoed with the clamour and the birds cried uneasily. Kishkar pattered on hurriedly, wanting to stand near Paramajoti.

While the grunting bearers lowered the bier on to the pyre of dry sticks and branches, the wailing of the women rose to a crescendo. The crowd swayed and groaned. Above this turbulence Paramajoti recited Sanskrit verses from a palm-leaf book. He extolled the glories of the after-life into which Sindavul had departed. He assured the people that she would receive safe conduct thanks to the buffalo spirit which would escort her to the threshold of the gods' domain.

Now fire had been set to the funeral pyre, which had been drenched in ghee. The dried foliage began to crackle. Blue smoke wreathed up in a swirling veil, as if to disguise from human sight the escape of Sindavul's spirit on its journey into the dark but desired unknown. The cries mingled with the roar of the all-consuming flames.

Kishkar felt weak and stifled. Leaving Tipane, in whose wide eyes triangles of flame were reflected, he turned and pushed his way through the scrimmaging crowd, ever pressing forward for a better view.

It was good to feel the soothing turf caressing his feet. As he ran he glanced up at the higher downland in the distance, hoping to be reassured by the sight of Moon Horn. But the young buffalo had vanished further into the hills and Kishkar felt leaden with unease. Tirelessly above the shimmering earth the vulture wheeled, as if transfixed for ever to the molten sky.

3 *Honour to the House*

Now the sun was sinking behind the hazy undulations of the Blue Hills. Already in the long shadows of the blue-gums and acacias the first trickles of night air were delicious as fresh water on the skin. The jackals were beginning their nightly dirge, like lost souls repenting their sins.

In the cattle-pounds the buffaloes were snorting and jostling, composing themselves for the night. They were not brought in every evening: often the herdsmen stayed out all night with them on the hills. But recently a tiger had raided the Hindu villages in the valley, so Kwodron and his neighbours had brought their cattle home for safety.

Outside the long, tunnel-shaped hut of bamboo and mud and wattles, Kishkar sat alone. His mind was restless, stirred and uneasy from the events of the day and his fears for Moon Horn. He felt uneasy but also elated, because of the possibility of being appointed Paramajoti's assistant.

"Come and play, Kishkar!" shouted one of the boys who were playing tip-cat near the well, but Kishkar only shook his head absently and did not answer.

"He is too proud!" jeered Kushken, hitting the lump of wood with the catstaff and making it fly in Kishkar's direction. "He is dreaming of the milking-brand on his right shoulder."

"The only mark Kushken will get on his shoulder is from the fleas he harbours!" retorted Tipane.

"Flea yourself!" Kushken yelled, whacking at Tipane with the catstaff. "You are small enough to be pinched out between finger and thumb."

The boys laughed and shouted and went scrambling after the tip-cat. Kishkar got up and moved out of their way. It was not because he was proud, but simply because his thoughts made him feel alone, shut off from the others. There was nothing he would have liked more than to join in their game; yet something held him back.

"Is my hair more beautiful than Laxam's, Kishkar?" demanded Sadamut, swaying gracefully as she padded past from the well with a chatti of water balanced on her glistening raven-wing hair.

"You use butter enough on it to feed ten thousand mouths," smiled Kishkar.

The shoulder of the earth had hunched up now, entirely dousing the light of the sun. The folds of the hills were covered in a dusting of delicate blue, like a strange, beautiful powder compounded from the colour of a dove's wing and the blossom of the jacaranda.

Now Kishkar stirred as he saw the women beginning to file away from the precincts of the dairy-temple, where Paramajoti had been distributing the milk and the buttermilk. Exactly like the dwelling-huts of the village, except that it was decorated with many holy signs, the temple was tunnel-shaped and under its projecting roof the dairy-priest stood. Bearded and venerable, he waited silently while the women withdrew, before returning to the sacred Buffalo Bell to fulfil the evening worship.

Gravely he returned Kishkar's distant salute, and Kishkar's step became more dignified, his shoulders stiffer, as he walked on. Perhaps soon, after a few days, he also would be allowed to set foot inside the temple. . . .

24

As the women, his mother among them, proceeded along the path, the brass chattis on their heads winking faintly in the fading light, Kishkar went over to the stone-walled cattle-pound, where the buffaloes contentedly chewed the cud from the rich pasture of the Blue Hills. There was never any lack of pasture for the buffalo. Day after day they grazed their fill, giving in return the bountiful milk on which their masters depended. The buffalo of the hills were a different race from the miserable, scrawny cows that tottered about the eroded fields of the plains, where the red soil vanished in sinister clouds of dust; or from the hairy water-buffaloes that shambled along dragging the plough.

Moon Horn had not yet lain down to rest. She stood by the wooden palisade, between the two stone gate-posts on which were carved the outline of a buffalo and the sign of the crescent moon and the midday sun. She stretched out her head in anticipation and Kishkar began with a smile to rub his knuckles along her muzzle. Moon Horn enjoyed this, and while Kishkar slowly and fondly rubbed the glossy hide, from which the flies had at last been driven by the keen air, the buffalo curled out her great tongue and licked the salty sweat on Kishkar's arm. Kishkar wriggled with delight as the rough, powerful tongue rasped over his skin.

"You're the finest buffalo in the Blue Hills," he murmured, as he rubbed Moon Horn's face. "Your eyes . . . they're more beautiful than pools of dew. Your horns are more splendid than the tusks of an elephant. . . ."

The heifer licked on complacently, as if she were accustomed to such compliments. Around her the other buffaloes sighed gustily and champed with tireless jaws.

Kishkar stared deep into those pools of eyes. How

terrible it would be if one day he saw them glaze over like the eyes of the slaughtered buffalo that morning. His nostrils quivered at the thought and he snatched away his hand as if that hideous notion might be transmitted through it to Moon Horn and upset her.

"I wouldn't wish to live without you, Moon Horn," Kishkar murmured, as he leaned on the carved gate-post. "If ever you were led to the death stone, I would go to. We'd go together into the shades. I wouldn't mind if we were together. But I would be afraid on my own. . . ."

While the buffalo heifer stretched out her chin and rubbed it on the top of the gate-post, Kishkar turned abruptly and hurried across the dew-soaked grass. The tropical dusk had descended like a sudden curtain. Fire-flies speckled the air with silver. It was time for the evening meal. The tip-cat game had broken up in shrill abuse, and Tipane came running home, still shouting defiance at Kushken, whose ancestry he described with remarkable vividness if not with accuracy. At the long tunnel hut he went down on hands and knees and crawled through the tiny, square doorway, hard on the heels of Kishkar.

Moutouvelli, mother of the house, squatted by the fire of dried cow-dung, preparing the dish of rice. She paused to put more life into the dull flames by blowing on them through a tube of bamboo. Kwodron had just lit the palm-oil lamp and as the brothers scrambled into the hut he stepped back to salute the light ceremonially, as he did without fail every eventide.

Now Laxam stooped on hands and knees through the low doorway. She poured water from a baked mud chatti over the outstretched hands of her father and brothers while Kwodron and Kishkar and Tipane squatted against

26

the raised stone platform, which took up half the space of the hut and on which presently the whole family would sleep, wrapped in their long cloaks.

They supped off rice kneaded into balls with coarse jaggery sugar and ghee, drank the rich butter-milk and enjoyed the paw-paws and sweet dwarf plantains and other fruit the Kothas had brought.

In the faint light of the palm-oil lamp, hardly stronger than the reflection from a moth's wings, Laxam's dark eyes gleamed. Her jet hair gleamed. The moonbeam flower in her hair gleamed. Her bare shoulder gleamed. Laxam wished to question her father, but she dared not. Her restlessness communicated itself to Moutouvelli, who did not keep quiet.

"Has Kunparadi spoken about our daughter and his son?" she asked Kwodron.

"He has spoken," nodded Kwodron, cupping rice in his hand. "But it will cost many buffaloes for the bribe. His animals are poorer than mine, yet I must give twice as many in return. But I shall ask him to count a chosen animal as two beasts. . . ."

"So much for a girl?" muttered Tipane. Fortunately for him he spoke through a mouthful of rice, so nobody heard what he said or he might have received harsh words to choke on.

Laxam sighed uneasily in the darkness, not knowing whether to be pleased or sorry to hear her fate being discussed and her dowry arranged. Kishkar frowned as he listened to his father. What did he mean by a chosen beast to count as two buffaloes? He did not like the sound of that. This was another hazard that might endanger Moon Horn, even if in a different way.

"What chosen buffalo would you pay Kunparadi with?" he asked, in an undertone, for he was diffident of evoking his father's anger. "The old bull or one of his sons would be good value."

"Leave this matter of your sister's dowry to me, my son," Kwodron answered sternly, though there was an understanding smile in the thickness of that night-black beard. "There are other things that concern you."

"The dairy-priest will appoint him . . ." Moutouvelli began, eagerly.

28

"Not so fast, woman," said Kwodron, raising a hand. "It is for the Council of the Elders to decide this. But Paramajoti has said that he wishes the boy to attend him at the festival tomorrow, to guard the temple precincts."

"Will he be branded then on the shoulder? Will it hurt him?" Tipane whispered to Laxam, who fed him with a ball of rice to stop his mouth.

Kishkar tried to control his breathing as he squatted there, but he tingled with pride. This was the first step to becoming the dairy-priest's acolyte . . . and that in turn would lead to his becoming the most honoured man among the People of the Buffalo one day.

"Our house will be greatly honoured," said Moutouvelli, in a respectful tone.

"The boy must act with pride and reverence," Kwodron went on, twitching his cloak about him. The white cotton garment seemed to emit more light than the palm-oil lamp itself. "Many people will be there. People from our other villages in the Blue Hills. Strangers from the valleys. Many will come to see the young men try their strength at the weight-lifting. There will be dancing, too. The wedding of Punog and Sotjabu. The Elders will meet in council. . . ."

"I will bear myself in seemly fashion," said Kishkar, in a voice that trembled a little, "and remember that I am my father's son."

"Do so at all times, then," Kwodron responded in his deep, dignified voice which contrasted with the high-pitched, eager chatter of his wife, from whom the words tumbled like a shower of tamarind fruit shaken down by monkeys. "All eyes will be watching to see how you bear yourself. The Elders will take note of whether you are worthy to have the milking-brand on your shoulder."

"There are jealous people, too," put in Moutouvelli, "who will be quick to say you are not dignified enough for the office."

"Kushken will get only a flea-bite on *his* shoulder," Tipane gleefully repeated his joke, but was ignored.

"Our son will be worthy of us," said Kwodron, in a voice like the distant rolling of surf on some ocean beach. His chest swelled, his massive shoulders were braced, for all this matter was of the utmost importance to a man of the People of the Buffalo. "Before the time comes for me to be led into the land of the shades I shall see my son become guardian of the sacred Buffalo Bell, leader of our people."

In the twilight of the palm-oil lamp Kishkar stared at the beaten earth floor of the hut. But his eyes saw other things than that.

4 *The Buffalo Bell*

SLOWLY, appraisingly, Teipakh settled his hands and arms round the immense spherical stone. It was no use making a sudden grab: the weight of the stone would simply pull you forward, head over heels, and roll back on your toes into the bargain. You had to coax the stone lovingly into your embrace, as if it were a living thing. You had to feel with your hands for the best grip, for some of the facets of the rock, worn by generations of aspirants in the contest, were smooth as glass.

The worst part was the first, raising the stone at all. It seemed as if you were lifting the whole earth, or, rather, that you would never succeed in lifting it. Mustering his strength, Teipakh felt that he was bending there for an eternity in front of the staring crowd who had gathered round to watch another man's effort.

Should he admit defeat, say he couldn't do it? This craven thought made Teipakh's muscles brace, his blood stir urgently. Never could he face the shame of that. It was not only that in order to qualify for any future death chase he must lift the stone; but he could never face the shame of admitting he was not strong enough to try.

While the hot sun glistened on his back and the spectators nudged and shuffled, Teipakh grappled with the stone. By the width of a blade of grass at a time the great ball of stone was rising. But at what a cost! Every nerve was

31

taut in pain, every muscle rippled. Teipakh's brown, fine-limbed body trembled as the ordeal began.

Now he must carefully lift one foot to the mounting-block, meanwhile gathering the stone up to his thighs. His breath began to shudder through his clenched teeth. The sweat trickled in oozy rivulets past his dilating eyes, into the hollows above the collar-bone, down over the starting furrows of his ribs. Slowly, his whole being quivering, he strove to conquer the weight. His body was drenched now as if by rain, his breath sang sharply like an adze on wood, his eyes bulged like a fish's. He could no longer see the ring of spectators grinning or looking grave according to their character. All he could see was the gauzy shimmer of trees and heat that seemed to change into a blank wall of red as he strove.

But he was conquering the stone, overcoming its terrible, inanimate strength that was more fearful than the struggle of a ravening animal, it sapped your strength so. Now he had eased it to his torso, where the banded muscles strained like bolts repelling a legion of intruders at a door.

Now he must lean back, legs braced, to heave the stone up to his shoulder. Now the crisis was approaching when Teipakh must prove himself or fail. The throng about him sensed the crisis. They had grown silent, unconsciously holding their breath: the Elders of the People of the Buffalo, who knew from experience what Teipakh was enduring; the young men whose turn to grapple with the stone would come; the mere spectators, Hindus from the market town in the valley, turbanned Badagas, white sahibs who had driven up to the hills in glittering, noisy machines that stank hotly. All shared, to however small an extent, in Teipakh's trial.

Carefully, one foot still braced on the mounting-block,

he leaned backwards as he manœuvred the stone over his chafed, naked chest. Not too far, for if you were not careful you would lose your balance and collapse while the vengeful stone crushed your ribs.

Now came Teipakh's supreme effort. For one brief heart-beat of a moment, he must hold the enormous stone poised while he gathered his last, utmost, proud strength for the final effort of putting it over his shoulder. His face was contorted, he was twenty years older than when he first took up the stone, his body shook like a man with palsy. Even the white sahibs in dark glasses and pith helmets folded their arms and ceased to smile cryptically.

Then it was done. Suddenly the stone moved ponderously through the air. Its hundred facets glinted dully as it turned, like the eye of a huge beast winking drowsily. Teipakh spun on his heels, moved away, and the gigantic ball of rock crashed down like a thrown wrestler as the earth round it shuddered.

Teipakh sagged, exhausted but victorious. The crowd relaxed, applauded a little, echoing Teipakh's sigh of relief, but soon began murmuring and shouting again, for they could not long keep silent. Down by the dairy-temple, in the shade of the rough stone wall of the precincts, Kishkar uttered a sigh of relief, too. He had watched Teipakh's efforts from a distance, suffered with Teipakh, trembled with him. Tipane, too, with effervescent enthusiasm, had kept his brother informed.

"Jadhav has failed . . . Teipakh has thrown the stone."

Tipane scurried to and fro between the trial-ring and the temple, partly to let his brother know, partly to let people know of his brother's important duty.

Kishkar breathed more easily again, glad that Teipakh had succeeded and, in raising the stone, had qualified for

34

the ritual of the death chase. He stirred as the people began to walk about again, strolling over the cushioned turf, curiously surveying the round-roofed dwellings and the palm-thatched temple. They chattered in Hindi or Malayalam or Tamil, and sometimes in English.

Kishkar would have liked to mingle with the throng, for he felt lonely here, guarding the temple. He envied the shouting and the laughter and the gossiping. But he knew his task was important and he stood with solemn dignity leaning on his staff when one of the tourists came towards him.

Politely Kishkar made namasta to him, saluting with hands pressed palms together in front of his face. The tourist, with a little smirk, replied in the same way. He must be very important, this white sahib, Kishkar knew, for he was a very large and stout man, fat enough to be a rajah, and was attended by an Indian bearer clad in pugree and khaki dress. His round black sun-glasses stared blankly out of his red face, which contrasted with the white of his crumpled drill suit.

The tourist's mem-sahib was important-looking, too, with her enormous hat and parasol. It was possible to tell that she was a mem-sahib because she was wearing a long frilly dress.

The tourist spoke meaninglessly to Kishkar, hoping to make him understand by broken words, like someone coaxing a dog with scraps of food. He pointed to the door of the temple and kept nodding and uttering single words.

"Let the sahib enter," ordered the bearer. "He will take off his shoes."

But shoes or no shoes, it was forbidden. Kishkar moved resolutely in front of the door without saying anything.

The tourist shrugged and grimaced, and spoke to his

mem-sahib, who smiled and surveyed Kishkar through spectacles that she held on a stick. Then he strolled away and took a black box that was hanging by a strap round his neck. Kishkar didn't understand how that black box worked, but he knew it would somehow make an image of anything it pointed at and was some sort of white sahib's magic. He believed this was harmless and felt it was not part of his duty to prevent it. So he watched indifferently while the white man peered and positioned, placed a hand over the top of the black box, pointed it at the temple and made something click.

Without another glance at Kishkar he walked casually along the slope above the temple, eyeing it appraisingly and taking more photographs. Once he made his mem-sahib stand in front of the temple. She straightened her hat and stood elegantly for him.

Presently a Hindu, dressed in a white cap and a white dhoti that trailed about his legs, and carrying an umbrella, got into conversation with them, gesticulating and laughing. Kishkar knew they were talking about the People of the Buffalo, for he could understand their tone even though he could comprehend only a few of the English words.

"They are certainly very quaint," said the tourist, while the mem-sahib drew disdainfully to one side.

"A vanishing people, my dear sir," the babu said shrilly. He gestured expansively to make certain everyone was aware that he was holding converse with a white sahib. "Fewer than one thousand survive, according to government statistics from census of last year, 1937 Anno Domini, as you say. It is said that they kill off their unwanted girl-children by putting them in the buffalo-pounds to be trampled on. . . ."

"They practise buffalo sacrifice also, I have read," said

the tourist, putting enough loftiness in his tone to keep the babu in his place. "Singularly uneconomic custom, one would think."

Kishkar was glad when they moved away beyond the temple.

Now the Dance of the Lords was beginning. The Kothas sat playing their vinegar-thin music while the Elders of the People, linking arms and brandishing their long staves, formed a circle. Rhythmically, ponderously as branches in a rising wind, the men performed the ceremonial dance. Step by slow step, arms linked tightly, staves held firmly upright, they moved in unison. First one way, then the other, round they pranced with dignity and nimbleness, rising on arched insteps which, even in the old men, were graceful and supple. The bunched muscles of their calves moved fluently as oiled machinery.

Once the dance had started, more and more men rushed forward to break into the circle which steadily expanded, while the Kotha pipes wailed respectfully and the shallow drums tapped out. Then the dancers began to chant an invocation to the sun and the moon, imploring nature to send goodness and calm and riches to the earth. They did not ask much, for the riches they had in mind were simply enough food to fill their bellies and enough cattle to pay their daughters' dowries when need be.

"Rhao! Rhao!" They punctuated the chant with guttural, fervent shouts and Kishkar watched eagerly as the stately ritual of the ring-dance proceeded.

All at once, from among the rhododendron trees beyond the little village, came a terrible scream. Like a stream frozen as it pours over a waterfall, all the chanting and the babbling of voices and the querulous music was cut off in a void of silence.

37

Tipane came running between the huts, shouting as he ran. He caught sight of Kishkar and hurried towards him, pallor evident even through the darkness of his skin.

"Sadamut!" he shrieked. "It is Sadamut! A snake!"

At once Kishkar ran to meet Tipane and together they went running back past the huts. Kishkar forgot all else in face of Sadamut's danger. Grasping his staff, he plunged through the gnarled bush-trees with their dense flowers. Others followed him, a shouting, eager mob, some aware of what was happening, the rest greedy for any sensation.

On the path stood Sadamut, transfixed, carrying a bundle of plantain leaves on her head. Beyond her, upright, tongue flickering, eyes glittering like agate, proud hood swelling, was a cobra. Swaying and menacing, it coiled there arrogantly, as if aware of its age-old domination over man. It hissed violently at the sound of pattering feet and started to glide towards the terrified Sadamut. But Kishkar did not pause to think. He seized the girl by the wrist so that she dropped her load and dragged her away along the path. Tipane picked up a stone, but thought better of it and with a wide-eyed glance over his shoulder at the cobra he went skipping hastily after his brother.

Now the crowd had come surging round, yelling advice, urging that the cobra be killed. But the cobra lay there defiantly, flickering out its black tongue in invitation. Many yelled boldly, but nobody wished to act. Nor did all men wish to slay the snake, for you never knew what gods you might offend in doing so.

At last this lowly creature which nature had caused to crawl upon its belly all its life, yet which all men feared, sank down, its hood with the celestial milk-blue rings deflated, and crept away into the depths of its mysterious haunts.

The people babbled more shrilly than ever. Men swore of the bold deeds they would have performed had they not been impeded. After much discussion everyone drifted back through the trees to continue the festival, for soon it would be time for the wedding of Punog and Sotjabu.

Somewhere a motor-car engine started its shattering noise, and the fat tourist with the red face went driving away along the dusty road beyond the village. His memsahib sat disapprovingly by his side, with a veil tied over her white hat. In the back seat the bearer sat with folded arms; he looked anxious . . . but maybe that was because the motor-car was a dangerous thing.

"Kishkar! Kishkar!" whispered Sadamut, her face still grey with fear. That was all she could say, but her deep brown eyes brimmed with gratitude.

"I must go back to the temple!" cried Kishkar, suddenly remembering his duty. Breaking away hurriedly, he threaded a path through the chattering throng.

As he came out on to the open pasture at the front of the dwelling-huts he saw Paramajoti burst out of the temple.

"He is angry with me for deserting my post," thought Kishkar, slowing to a more dignified walk. "I must explain . . ."

But there was no question of explanation. The old man's usually tranquil features were contorted with rage as he came towards Kishkar, brandishing his staff and crying out. At first Kishkar could not take in his words, for Paramajoti was almost incoherent in his agitation. Then they sank in and Kishkar came to a halt, as if a fist had been driven into his face. The whole world seemed to melt away round him. He stood there in unbelieving horror.

"The Buffalo Bell!" Paramajoti was shouting, his face

ravaged by fury. "The sacred bell has been stolen! Jackal, carrion, worthless reproach to your father, you have failed in your duty. Better you had never been born or that the buffalo had trampled you at birth. Shame on the woman who bore you. . . ."

The Buffalo Bell! The sacred Buffalo Bell stolen! The temple violated—in those few minutes while he had left the precincts. People came running, shouting, gesturing angrily. Paramajoti's wrathful words were tossed on the air, spat from the mouth like splashes of bitter juice. Even an earthquake could not have caused such confusion.

Hollow with shame, hardly aware of the angry hands that pushed him, the grimacing faces that crowded round him, Kishkar stood there staring as the outraged priest raised his staff to strike.

"Don't beat my brother!" Tipane pleaded at the edge of the crowd. "It was the snake, it was the snake!"

"Beating is not enough," voices shouted. "No thrashing will atone for the theft of the bell!"

Down towards the valley trailed a column of dust as a motor-car made its leisurely way among the winding brakes of bamboo and blue-gum and acacia.

5 For Moon Horn's Sake

SOMEWHERE in a fold of the hills, where the shadows of the camphire shrubs and the gorse bushes advanced furtively like outposts of night, a painted partridge uttered its insistent, creaking call, *chick-chick-cheray, chick-chick-cheray.* Again and again it sent up its call, unsatisfactory as a blunt knife carving stone.

The rusty, monotonous cry found an echo in Kishkar's mind. For all the time a persistent thought had kept reminding him of the previous day's shame. The Buffalo Bell, the sacred Buffalo Bell, precious above all else to the People of the Buffalo, had been stolen. The temple had been violated. Not even the People themselves were permitted to enter that holy place, yet now it had been uncouthly broken into by an unclean foreigner whose gods —if he had any—were not those of Kishkar's people. And this outrage, which had sundered the leisurely peace of the Blue Hills and turned the people grave-faced and wondering, as at the death of some great person, all this was Kishkar's fault.

As he squatted there, staring unseeing at the blue mantle of another evening as it spread across the hills, his whole slim body seemed to burn at the memory of the shame he had endured. It was as if the words of abuse and reproach that the men and the boys had shouted at him had actually, physically, burned him. Not only his mind, but all his body, felt sore and beaten from the invisible scourge of shame.

And added to the stinging pain of this was the salt of injustice. He couldn't understand why it had all happened. Why should that gross white man, fat-bellied and aloof, need to steal the sacred bell? What did it mean to him, if his gods were different?

Why, too, should it have happened simply because Kishkar heard that Sadamut was in danger and had gone to her aid? If he had ignored the girl's cry, none of this would have happened. But Sadamut might be dead, struck by the cobra. Maybe the gods would have had it so. Was Sadamut's death of less consequence than the theft of the Buffalo Bell?

Miserable almost to the point of indifference, still stunned by what had happened, Kishkar sat huddled staring at the blue void of the hills. From the pride of anticipation he had been cast down as devastatingly as a bird in full song might be struck by a falcon. He had brought shame to his father, sorrow to his mother and anger and dismay to the People.

He did not stir when he heard a light footstep over the downland turf, but he sensed that the newcomer was Sadamut. She did not approach him direct but presently came and squatted a little way to one side and behind him.

For a long time the boy and the girl sat in apparent silence, yet during this muteness invisible messengers passed between them as surely as if they were exchanging words.

Chick-chick-chick-cheray, the painted partridge called, and the hill slopes threw back his voice so that it seemed as though a dozen birds were creaking out their evening gossip.

"I have brought you food," Sadamut said timidly after

42

a while. "It's very little. Some korali grain and some honey and paw-paws. I know you haven't eaten all day, for Laxam told me."

She rose and placed the food, which she had brought wrapped in plantain leaves, near Kishkar's right hand, then returned to where she had been sitting.

"I was ashamed to return to my father's house," Kishkar muttered. "But I was not afraid."

"What will you do?" Sadamut whispered, bowing her head with its long, sleek tresses that reached over her shoulders. She had not buttered her ringlets today, nor even put a flower in her hair.

"It's not for me to decide," shrugged Kishkar, kneading some of the korali in his fingers. He laughed humourlessly. "They will have to appoint another acolyte to the priest. Your brother's shoulder must be itching now. Tipane laughed too soon."

"Kushken is bad," said Sadamut, her dark eyes hooded. "He has sneered all day and made a song of how you guarded the temple."

"What do the People say about me?"

"They say Kwodron will be made to pay a large fine. The Council of the Elders is meeting now. Everyone is shouting. It was like a storm. Paramajoti is to make a speech."

"What gods do the white men believe in?" Kishkar frowned. "Why should that white sahib need to steal the Buffalo Bell? Did he wish to take it as a tribute to his gods?"

"It would have been better had I been killed by the snake," said Sadamut, twisting the bangle on her wrist. "I could cut out my tongue because it was my scream that brought shame to you."

"But now you have brought food to me instead,"

43

Kishkar answered, almost gaily. He was fond of Sadamut and did not like to see her sad.

"Someone is coming!" Sadamut exclaimed fearfully, and they started to get up as two figures appeared across the grassy slope, outlined against the sky.

"It is Laxam and Tipane with her," murmured Kishkar, resting on one knee and eyeing his sister intently. There was something urgent in Laxam's appearance as the girl hurried towards them, and Tipane's lips were parted as if to shout. "What news?" Kishkar demanded, standing up, as Laxam, clutching her white robe about her, came breathlessly nearer.

"The Council of the Elders has met," Laxam panted, a hand to her breast. "They have sat all day in the meeting-glade. Teipakh warned me. He heard them when they started back to their villages. . . ."

"What have they decided?" Sadamut asked, in a stifled voice, her eyes searching Laxam's.

"They say it is as if a death had occurred. . . ."

"Yes, how can they say that? What do they mean?" Tipane asked.

"A death?" frowned Kishkar, plucking at his robe, for the chill of evening was diluting the air. "I don't understand."

"The theft of the Buffalo Bell," Laxam went on. She spoke more evenly now, yet still gravely. "Paramajoti said this was worse than death to the People of the Buffalo and that a fitting sacrifice would be needed to atone for it."

Still Kishkar did not or would not understand what his sister meant. Yet, somehow the chill that was tingling on his body also began to clutch at his heart.

"They will make Kwodron pay?" Sadamut asked, her voice quiet as the voice of a shadow.

44

"Yes," Laxam nodded, watching her brother, for she knew what it would mean to him. "Kwodron must pay with his best buffalo. It must be led to the death stone."

"Moon Horn?" cried Kishkar: and he experienced a kind of pain as the cry was torn from him.

He had never before uttered that name to the two girls or his brother, but they knew what he meant. They were all aware of how precious the buffalo heifer was to him. They knew also how valuable she was because of her ancient lineage.

"Yes," said Laxam. "The council has decreed it. The heifer has the sacred mark on her tail and is therefore Kwodron's most valuable beast. Our father has accepted the decision."

Tipane's eyes were large as he stared up at his brother. He sank down on his haunches as if to avoid Kishkar's anger.

Kishkar glanced round wildly. His nostrils quivered. His dark eyes were alight for the first time that day.

"Have the herdsmen gone to bring in the cattle?" he asked, sharply.

"Not yet," Tipane told him, venturing to stand up again. "Nobody has done anything today. It has been like a festival. But not happy like a festival," he added, his face clouding.

"All the people have waited to hear the decision of the Council," said Laxam. "They have talked of nothing but the theft of the sacred bell."

"There is still time, then," said Kishkar, as if to himself. He began to move away. His stride lengthened as his resolution hardened.

"Where are you going? What will you do, Kishkar?" Laxam and Sadamut watched him anxiously.

"Don't be afraid!" he reassured them, breaking into a run. "But tell nobody of where I have gone."

"I will come with you!" cried Tipane, running after him.

"No!" Kishkar shouted fiercely over his shoulder. "Go back with the girls. You must obey me."

Without another glance at Laxam and Sadamut, who stood white-clad in the swiftly gathering blue twilight, Kishkar hurried away over the downs. He was not quite certain what he was going to do. His heart beat with determination and fearfulness. It was a terrible thing to set out deliberately to flout the word of the Elders, but how much worse to allow Moon Horn to be sacrificed because of his own shame! He must save the heifer. That was all that mattered. He would rather be condemned to the shades himself than allow the innocent Moon Horn to suffer the penalty of Kunparadi's sledge-hammer.

As he went loping up one of the slopes and emerged on

to a high crest, he could hear the sound of voices in the distance. The men were shouting to one another as they set out to herd the buffaloes back to the village pounds.

There was still time, but he must hurry. The dove-blue mantle of the hills was already turning to the colour of a crow's wing. He was uneasy at the thought of being out at night and it was not only the effort of running that made his chest heave.

Under his feet a partridge exploded in a churr of wings and went spinning off into the dusk. In the distance jackals were wailing.

He knew where he would find Moon Horn, as the buffalo had their regular pattern of grazing. The herd snorted and moved off a little as Kishkar approached; not really in fright but because they wanted to prolong the moment of being driven from their pasture. They circled round, reassured by the familiar rancid butter smell of Kishkar's robe.

"Moon Horn!" the boy called, wanting the heifer to recognize his voice. "It's me, Kishkar, your friend. Don't be afraid."

He walked quietly up to the buffalo, who put out her head towards him and then resumed her feeding, while the other animals milled round and breathed grassily.

"We must go away, Moon Horn," Kishkar said, putting a hand on the heifer's neck and feeling the strength of her muscles as she grazed. Moon Horn turned to go reluctantly in the accustomed direction, back to Kishkar's village. Beyond the ridge the voices grew louder.

It was difficult to persuade Moon Horn to go where Kishkar wanted. She was not used to being separated from the herd, yet at the same time she was so trusting of the boy that gradually she allowed him to lead her away through

47

one of the meadowy cleaves which ran down towards the river.

By now the voices were nearer and more agitated, as if someone had guessed what Kishkar was about. For undoubtedly the herdsmen would first make sure that Moon Horn was brought in. The word of the Elders must be carried out.

Kishkar recognized Kushken's voice and he made Moon Horn hurry. He knew that above all Kushken would gloat at his downfall and would want to see his shame completed by the sacrifice of Kwodron's most valuable animal.

By now the brief twilight was over as if at the blink of an eye; but the darkness that followed was as brief. The vast arched ceiling of the sky was soon lambent with stars that diffused a ghostly, dreamlike radiance over the hills. In turn, their loveliness would be dimmed by the huge gourd of the moon that was already swinging up in the east.

Kishkar had no time to be afraid or even cold in the sudden onset of night air. He was intent only on escaping with Moon Horn. He had no notion where he was going. He must simply go. Kishkar and the young buffalo hurried on down the cleave in the pallid light, brushing through grass that was cold and clinging with dew. The voices of the herdsmen were more distant now. Evidently most of the men and youths had started to herd the rest of the buffaloes away towards the village, perhaps assuming that Moon Horn was among them as usual.

But Kishkar knew he was not safe yet. He knew that someone was following him. Furtively, swiftly, implacably, someone was following him, skulking among the gorse bushes whose flowers filled the thin air with little breaths of fragrance. Kishkar could hear nothing but the

48

sound of his own and Moon Horn's going and now the rustle of water ahead of them. Nevertheless, the hint of those pursuing footsteps thudded in his mind.

It must be Kushken who was dogging him—the jealous Kushken, who was not content with Kishkar's shame, but sought to complete the process of his mortification.

"But he will not! He shall not!" Kishkar thought, as he ran on alongside Moon Horn, who by now had realized the urgency of what was happening.

Now Kishkar had to think fast, for in his eagerness to get away he had forgotten the stream. The splash and murmur of water grew louder, the starlight glimmered on the dancing surface. They had come to the hill stream that flowed down the tortuous ravines towards the great river of the plains. The stream was not wide, but it might be difficult to cross at night among the fern-bowered rocks.

With a hand on Moon Horn's flank, Kishkar came to a halt, pondering which way to go. They had come to the edge of a pool in the stream where the buffalo often drank. Now the pursuing footsteps were undeniable. Vague as a half-formed thought, a figure took shape in the dimness. Kushken came running down hard to take advantage of Kishkar's hesitancy.

Kishkar struck Moon Horn on the flank to send her away along the stream, then he turned with a defiant cry to meet Kushken. The two boys grappled in a welter of limbs and the force of the encounter sent them rolling over on the ground.

The fall drove the breath from Kishkar with a spurting gasp. He was hampered by his cotton robe, while his opponent was naked but for his loin-cloth and could more easily fight. Kushken's body was slippery as polished wood: it was as if each limb were a separate entity on its own, each one a different assailant.

Silent but for their desperate breathing, the two boys struggled for mastery. Furiously Kishkar strove to throw off Kushken and at first it felt as if his strength were deserting him. It seemed that Kushken would prevail; Kishkar could sense the exultation in him.

Now other footsteps were coming through the night: someone else was coming to Kushken's aid. Bitterly Kishkar tried to free himself before this fresh assault. Out of the darkness a small figure appeared. Kushken gasped noisily as the newcomer half stumbled, half flung himself on the opponents.

It was Tipane. Shouting breathlessly, he was no match for Kushken, but the diversion gave Kishkar an opportunity to recover. While Kushken turned savagely to deal with Tipane, Kishkar rolled free, seized Kushken by the arms and threw him with all his strength.

Vainly Kushken tried to recover, but the sloping bank gave him no purchase. With a cry of rage he went slithering head first down the trampled ground where the buffalo came to drink and the water cascaded out in brief white lacework as he fell into the pool.

Bruised and panting but elated, Kishkar stood watching Kushken floundering in the water. Tipane ran to his side, uncertain whether to laugh with triumph or cry because of the grievous blow Kushken had dealt him.

"Cool your valour awhile, Kushken-son-of-a-jackal!" he shrieked, clenching his small fists and dancing from one foot to the other. He picked up the nearest thing to hand, a ball of dried cattle-dung, and flung it at Kushken as he was scrambling out of the water. It landed on the boy's shoulder and made him lose his balance so that he slithered back again into the stream. Even Kishkar could not help laughing at Kushken's discomfiture.

But there was no time for laughing. Gathering his muddied robe about him and seizing Tipane with his other hand, Kishkar hastened away into the night to find Moon Horn.

6 Land of Strangers

ALONG the breathless road where the red dust smoked through the billowing foliage of the tamarinds, people sauntered to and fro, languid in the heat. Women in shimmering green saris, gold studs in their noses, strolled with baskets on their hips, gathering cow-dung for fuel. A convoy of tiny, frail pack-donkeys tottered past with bowed heads, laden with skin bags of palm-toddy or sacks of grain. A man sat asleep with knees up to his chin on a creaking cart while the weary bullocks hauled it along on its solid wooden wheels.

Stunned by the heat, deafened by insects, Kishkar squatted in the shelter of the elegant, plumey bamboos above the road. He stared and listened and wondered. Never before had he heard or smelt or seen anything like this. From the open freshness and solitude of the Blue Hills he and Tipane and Moon Horn had descended in a mere day or two into another world, a world of blatant colour that screamed like noise—and strident noise that seemed like a medley of colours . . . and of pungent scents that were not all aromatic.

The river down beyond the huts and the green-tinged paddy-fields was different, sluggish and ugly as if some monster had been churning up its depths. Even the air was different. Instead of the pure air of the hills, as refreshing as some cool invigorating draught, the air down here in the valley was like a dirty rag that brushed against your face. The never-ending red dust which oozed from the ugly wounds of the crumbling earth clogged your skin and made your eyes smart.

Your ears, too, were constantly assailed. The everlasting clatter and sizzling of the cicadas was like the noise of the earth frying in the heat. In the trees the birds were never quiet. Chattering parakeets and gossiping minivets, raucous drongos and self-opinionated mynahs: the branches were alive with gaudy wings and strident voices. The birds of the tropics did not sing; their colours sang instead.

Kishkar shifted uneasily and waved a bamboo frond above the sleeping Tipane to drive away the flies. He wished he could drive away the cicadas and their maddening din. You couldn't even think because of those cicadas. The sweat tickled him as it ran down his naked back, for he had taken off his embroidered robe and used it only at night when he and Tipane slept underneath it. They had been comforted by the heavy tang of the rancid butter Moutouvelli had rubbed in it to make it waterproof. The smell reminded the brothers of the Blue Hills.

Kishkar touched the bundled cotton garment fondly, as if to reassure himself and then glanced round into the trees where Moon Horn was grazing as best she could. He was worried about the buffalo heifer, for the grazing was poor and dust-choked down here—no wonder the cattle that he had watched were so weak and listless—and the insects troubled her unceasingly, so that she stamped her hooves irritably and twitched her glossy hide in impatient ripples.

Kishkar was worried, too, about Tipane. He swished the flies away again from his brother's shining face as Tipane slept there curled at his side, his small hands clutched over his belly as if to assuage the hunger he felt. Tipane couldn't understand what was happening. After the first spice of adventure had lost its flavour he could see no reason for lingering in this land of strangers.

Kishkar longed to go back to the Blue Hills as much as Tipane did. He had never ventured half as far from home before. He found it difficult to believe that only the day before yesterday he had still been there, breathing the fragrance of blue-gum and gorse, his feet caressed by the soft rich grass. He seemed to be in some terrible dream in which he wandered ever further from his homeland. If only he could wake up from that dream! But he dared not return. For though down here in this strange land there was only hunger and loneliness for him and Tipane, back at home there was only shame for himself . . . and death for Moon Horn. He had committed an unspeakable crime, too, in flaunting the decision of the Elders.

He groaned as he thought of the terrible emptiness that faced him. He looked down at Tipane again as he protected his brother from the flies. Could he ever make him understand?

He groaned again as he thought how hungry he was. They had eaten so little since leaving home. Yesterday, a family of wandering basket-makers, cutting bamboo stems with razor-sharp knives, had taken pity on them and let them share their meal, for they were low caste, as were the People of the Buffalo in Hindu eyes. That morning Kishkar had gathered a few handfuls of tamarind dates and had found a fallen coconut from which he and Tipane had drunk the milk, but that was all. Food was hard to come by in a land where people were used to going hungry.

Now Kishkar intended to wait until sunset, and when the villagers had brought home their scrawny cattle he would have to brave the barking pariah dogs and try to take some fruit.

Screened by the trees from the passers-by a stone's throw away, he squatted quietly, enduring the heat and the flies and his burning hunger. Occasionally he turned to make certain Moon Horn had not strayed too far or to fan the bamboo frond over the huddled Tipane. But presently even that became too much of an effort. His head lolled painfully and however much he tried he could not prevent his eyelids from closing. Kishkar slept.

But not for long. All at once he felt Tipane tugging anxiously at his hand and at the same time he heard a snorting and a trampling of hooves. He sprang up alertly, for he knew that something had alarmed Tipane and Moon Horn.

"It is a devil who wants to steal Moon Horn," Tipane whispered fearfully, pressing close against his brother. A man was standing not far away, peering from the shelter of a stinkwood tree at the heifer, who was restively pawing the earth. The stranger was naked except for a loin-cloth and a dirty pugree round his head. His glistening skin was as black as coal and his mouth was red as a devil's from chewing betel-nut.

Kishkar clutched the stick he had cut for a staff and hurried to Moon Horn's side. Tipane paused just long enough to pick up a stone and hurried after him.

"That is a fine animal you have," the man remarked, eyeing the two brothers furtively as he emerged from behind the tree. He spat a long stream of red juice. "Where did you steal her?"

Kishkar watched him but did not reply. His hand tightened on his staff. Tipane scowled impressively and raised his stone.

"I will buy her from you," the man said, sidling nearer. In his dark face his dark black eyes moved like watchful beasts at the threshold of their lair. His lips were hot-looking as vicious flame.

"She is not for sale," Kishkar replied. He was not sure what to do, for though the man was alone he had come from the village and could call on other men to help him.

But Moon Horn settled things. The heifer sniffed the air and did not like the smell of this stranger. She pawed the earth again, shook her tall horns and advanced towards the man. The man turned and made off. He was un-accustomed to such boldness—his own cattle were too feeble and starved ever to resist. But his eyes were greedy as he glanced back at Moon Horn, and he raised a threatening hand as Tipane flung the stone to speed him on his way.

"If you will do business," he shouted at Kishkar, "ask for Choran Woodcutter. . . ."

"We must not go to sleep again," Kishkar said, when the man had disappeared. "We must guard Moon Horn well and when evening comes I will find some food."

"Why can't we go home?" demanded Tipane, as Kishkar led Moon Horn further into the trees. "There is plenty of food there and people won't want to steal Moon Horn from us."

"They would do worse than steal Moon Horn," Kishkar muttered, while he sat wearily against a tree and wondered when the brass gong in the sky would stop beating.

At last the whining drone of a cattle horn in the distance confirmed that the sun was relenting. The lengthening shadows seemed to be trying to smother the smoke of dust that had drifted all day as if from a fire that was slowly consuming the earth. Ugly and mud-plastered, the water-buffaloes lurched back from the fields. In a shuffling patter of hooves, the emaciated, hump-shouldered, dewlapped cows were driven home by almost naked boys.

Kishkar marvelled as he watched this shambling procession of animals which hardly had the strength to ring the bells round their meagre necks. He pitied the people who owned such ill-looking beasts and shuddered at the thought that Moon Horn might be afflicted by the starvation that beset the village cattle.

From the huddle of thatched huts rose the smoke of cattle-dung fires as women prepared the evening meal. Kishkar avoided Tipane's disconsolate glance as they caught the smell of curried rice. His mouth would have watered but it was too parched. When he swallowed it was as if he had a mouthful of flints.

"Listen, Tipane," said Kishkar, when he decided the time had come. "You must wait here for me with Moon Horn. If anyone comes, drive her further into the jungle and wait. . . ."

"I want to come with you," Tipane begged. "Only because I am hungry. I'm not afraid," he added stoutly.

"Stay and guard Moon Horn," Kishkar ordered. "I will come back soon and we will eat."

While the cicadas sizzled and the crickets shrilled and countless other voices screeched or ticked or boomed, he crept down nearer the village, skulking from tree to tree until he stood under the swaying avenue of tamarinds. At the end of the village the dun-coloured river wound sluggishly, like some distended reptile crawling away from a feast. The slanting rays of the sun redeemed its sinister appearance by embellishing it with flecks of gold. In mid-stream a tall grey rock stood like an old elephant sitting in the water. On the rock several pelicans perched, wings trailing, pouches bulging, as they digested their supper. On a sandbank a strange log-like object seemed to stir vaguely, as if disturbed by the wash of the river.

Its hub-bells tinkling, a bullock-cart was trundling across the sagging wooden bridge that spanned the river. When it had passed, Kishkar made his way into an orange grove bordering the river. As he flitted across the road he noticed a little shrine made of rough slabs of stone. It was tiny, too small for a man to enter standing up, and was flanked by prancing terracotta horses. But what interested Kishkar was a pile of fruit, oranges and plantains and tree-tomatoes, which the villagers had left there.

He halted, gazing hungrily at this ready-made meal. It would have been so easy, but he must not give in to the temptation. The fruit had been brought as an offering to propitiate the local gods and he would be committing a dire sin if he stole it. The eyes of the terracotta horses bulged, their nostrils flared, as they pranced endlessly on guard.

Sternly Kishkar suppressed the sacrilegious promptings of his belly and hurried along the edge of a paddy-field towards the orange grove. The fruit hung there like so many gay lanterns and there was plenty of it. Surely it wouldn't matter if he helped himself to assuage his own and Tipane's hunger? After all, the fruit bats would soon flock down and boldly raid the oranges. Perhaps he should stay behind and scare off some of the fruit bats in order to make up for the fruit he took. . . .

Quickly he bent down a branch of one of the little trees and picked several of the brilliant, loose-skinned fruit. He pouched them in the folds of his rolled-up cloak, which he had been carrying on his shoulder, and then tied up the ends of the cloak with liana stems.

Would it be greedy to eat just one of the oranges before he went back to Tipane? As he hesitated a scavenging pariah dog came loping past. It scuttled away at the sight of a stranger but, lifting its miserable snout, began to bark urgently. Kishkar threatened it with a stick, but this only made the animal howl more desperately. From somewhere beyond the trees a man shouted at it to be quiet.

Kishkar crept away silently, the oranges joggling on his shoulder. The dog circled near him, howling and yelping. Soon other dogs began to bark on the outskirts of the village and Kishkar quickened his pace.

"Who is there?" shouted the man. "If it is Kallo stealing my fruit I will thrash him until he squeals for mercy!"

"Suktan, you say that to hide your own thefts!" another man, no doubt the one named Kallo, shouted back. "If the zamindar looked in your cooking-pot he would find his goat the tiger was blamed for taking!"

"I am no low-caste eater of flesh!"

"By my eye, though, you will become an eater of words —your own!"

The altercation continued while the men drew nearer. Some of the other villagers emerged from their huts to make certain their crops were not being pilfered. The pariah dog continued to shrill at Kishkar. Then somebody caught sight of the boy. Kishkar knew that concealment was useless any longer. He went running through the orange grove while a hubbub of anger broke out behind him. Along the raised bunds that divided the paddy-fields men came hurrying in pursuit, their white shirts and dhotis flapping.

Once again Kishkar found himself in desperate flight,

this time from hostile strangers who would beat him for a thief. Thumped by the oranges, he stumbled on through the plantation, wondering how he was going to escape. At the edge of the trees he found he was not far from the wooden bridge. The best thing would be to get away across the river and try to rejoin Tipane later on when the hue and cry had died down.

But as he turned along the river bank he caught sight of someone running towards him from the bridge. It was Choran Woodcutter, the same villager who had cast envious eyes on Moon Horn earlier in the day. Kishkar's escape was cut off. He came to a halt, breathing deeply, fists clenched, while Choran hurried on towards him, his red mouth uttering abuse. To Kishkar's left the rest of the villagers ran, accompanied by the pariah dogs, intent on surrounding him. Kishkar turned and sped along the river shore where the village dhobi-man's laundry lay spread out to dry. Now to his dismay he saw Tipane and Moon Horn at the edge of the river. Evidently Moon Horn had needed to drink and Tipane had been unable to stop her. The heifer had waded out a few yards among the reeds and was gratefully sucking up even that turbid water.

Alarmed by the commotion, Moon Horn trampled away out of the river, while Tipane scuttled after her.

"No, Tipane!" Kishkar cried as he ran. "We must cross the river!"

The mob of villagers was hard behind him. In a few moments they would seize him. They would take possession of Moon Horn and would thrash Kishkar and Tipane unmercifully. Not even when Kushken pursued him vengefully had Kishkar run so fast. The blood pounded in his ears; the sweat covered his body in a greasy film.

He drove Moon Horn back towards the river. Bewildered but obedient, the buffalo waded out into the deepening water. Kishkar grabbed his brother's hand, then lifted him up and swung him astride Moon Horn. Kishkar himself was soon thigh-deep, waist-deep, struggling now. He caught hold of the heifer's tail with one hand and floundered along, spluttering and gasping, half swimming, half dragged, impeded by his bundle of oranges. Tipane had ceased to yell and clung on tightly to Moon Horn who, her chin stretched out, her muzzle cleaving the water, had settled into a steady pace across the river.

Now they were safe, or so it seemed, for the villagers had come to a halt on the shore, chattering and yelling, trampling the once clean laundry. But their clamouring tone changed abruptly, and even the dhobi-man, who was screeching in rage at so much work being spoilt, paused with open mouth. Everyone had grown unaccountably and ominously silent.

At first Kishkar was too busy struggling through the water to take any notice. Then, as he heaved himself up, trying to get on the heifer's back as well, he drew in his breath with a hiss of consternation. On the sandbank across the river the log-like object had woken up. A long snout was rippling into the water, followed by an even longer, armoured tail.

7 *The God in the River*

KISHKAR prayed to his gods, to the great god Ouen and to
Pinakurs, Ouen's wife, who was equally powerful, to the
sun and the moon, to any gods he could think of in his
predicament. Not even the journey to the Shades could
be fraught with such terror as this crossing of the river, and
Kishkar implored the gods to deliver Tipane and himself
from danger. At the same time he desperately urged
Moon Horn forward, clinging to her tail, like the first of
the People of the Buffalo when he was dragged out of the
mountainside. His hand found a secure grip on the
pedigree kink in the heifer's tail.

Tipane, too, sitting on her shoulders, drummed Moon
Horn with his heels to make her swim faster, but the
buffalo could only struggle slowly against the weight of
the water and the encumbrance of her passengers. Her

gaping nostrils blew strenuously, her sides heaved with the unaccustomed effort, and her eyes bulged not only with the strain but because she was imbued with some of the boys' terror. She knew that danger lurked in those sombrous waters.

On the shore the villagers had regained their voices and were discussing the situation animatedly. More people had hurried down from the village, women and children and old folk. The villagers knew the perils of the river only too well, for until the flimsy bridge was built the crossing had been full of hazards. Even now the crocodile occasionally ambushed an unwary dhobi-man, or a child who had driven the cattle down to drink. Only strangers would be foolish enough to cross the river like this.

With difficulty Kishkar clung to the buffalo's tail, while the water slopped round his head. He could not see the crocodile, but he knew only too well from the blurred shouts of the villagers that it was paddling towards this unexpected offering. The river was not wide—a boy could fling a stone across it if he tried—but now, however much Moon Horn struggled and blew, the opposite bank seemed to draw no nearer.

None the less they were gradually making progress, for now the tall grey rock that looked like an elephant's head was quite close, and that was more than half way. On it the pelicans sat replete, their enormous beaks still crammed with fish, their wings trailing.

"Faster, Moon Horn, faster!" Tipane begged, slapping the buffalo's side. He had been trying to stare straight ahead but now his fear-brimmed eyes were drawn in the crocodile's direction. To his horror he saw a sinister fluting in the water and in his agitation made Moon Horn lurch violently, so that Kishkar lost his grip on her tail.

63

Choking, swallowing the evil-looking water, hampered by the oranges, Kishkar struggled to save himself. He tried to splutter at Tipane to wait for him, but the river stopped his mouth and Moon Horn paddled on. Tipane, unaware of what had happened to his brother, tucked up his heels and clung more desperately than ever to the horns of the buffalo.

Kishkar floundered in the swirling water, expecting at any moment to feel the jaws of the crocodile closing on his helpless body. His limbs were clumsy with fear and a host of images passed before his eyes. He could see Moutouvelli and Sadamut and Laxam, dimly, far away: it was as if they were trying to help him, holding out their hands to bring him to safety.

The thought of them made him struggle fiercely and he fought his way to the surface. Never had a more joyful sight greeted him, for through a veil of water he saw the rock looming close ahead, grey and impassive. Unaware of the bruises on his legs, he clambered on to it, dragged himself up its smooth, slippery sides that were streaked with pelican droppings. Not till he reached the topmost dome of the rock did he dare to pause and look down at the river.

The crocodile was already there. The water boiled, angrily, hideously, as the crocodile thrashed about in frustration. It had been so sure of its victim that it had taken things a little too slowly. Its eyes glowed dull, resentful red as Kishkar stared down into them, and its jagged, warty tail curved menacingly to and fro, ready to sweep him round within reach of those nightmare jaws, should he lose his hold on the rock.

Trembling, Kishkar leaned over cautiously to watch the monster churning only a few feet below him. He had not known that anything so terrifying could exist. Round him the pelicans shuffled and jostled uneasily, vaguely worried at this invasion of their sanctuary, but they were far too full of fish to stir.

In the twilight, the watching villagers still clustered on the shore. Their tone had changed to one of anger again. They appeared as disappointed as the crocodile that Kishkar had escaped. To them the crocodile was by way of being a god and it was desirable that he should be appeased from time to time. What better way of achieving this than for a stranger to oblige?

But Kishkar had only escaped for the time being. He had still to cross to the other shore. Only now did he think of Tipane and Moon Horn. Quickly he looked round for them and saw with relief that Moon Horn was emerging from the river, with Tipane scampering round, urging her to hurry.

Relieved though he was, Kishkar now felt more isolated than ever. How could he possibly escape? He shivered as he imagined the crocodile besieging him all night on that bare rock, prowling about in the water, waiting for him to fall asleep—and lose his grip. Or perhaps the crocodile would exert some evil power over him with those baleful red eyes in the top of that fearful head.

Kishkar felt weak and lonely as he lay there. The on-coming night clattered and racketed with the sound of insects and frogs and birds and the surfeited pelicans gurgled and shuffled. It really seemed as if the gods must disapprove of him if they could let him come to this sorry pass.

First he had been disgraced at home in the Blue Hills because he had gone to the help of Sadamut, and now he was in dire peril simply because he had been hungry. Surely he would not be sacrificed to the crocodile merely because he had helped himself to a few oranges? He thought bitterly of how different his present situation was compared with the proud future he had anticipated only a few evenings ago. Surely the crocodile hadn't been sent because he had flouted the decision of the Elders and refused to allow Moon Horn to be taken to the death stone?

Kishkar blinked rapidly as he gazed down at the dim shape of the crocodile patrolling near the foot of the rock. Perhaps it would be better to end his agony now and plunge down into those cruel jaws, instead of enduring hours of fear and uncertainty.

Kishkar was distracted from his troubles by the sight of Choran Woodcutter running across the bridge—he still had envious eyes for the buffalo heifer. Other villagers began to follow Choran, eager to share the spoils.

"Tipane!" yelled Kishkar, clambering to his feet so that the pelicans squawked anxiously. "Run! They are coming to steal Moon Horn!"

But in his excitement Tipane did not know what to do and stood wavering on the bank while Moon Horn bellowed, not understanding why Kishkar was not there. Kishkar was so angry at the greed of the villagers that he forgot his fear of the crocodile: the anger made his blood hot and he felt better. Yet there was nothing he could do. Even if he escaped from the river he would have lost Moon Horn. The villagers would take possession of the heifer and swear she was their property. They would subject Moon Horn to all sorts of indignities and soon make her thin-ribbed as any village cow.

But Moon Horn had no intention of dragging a plough or an ox-cart, and as the woodcutter tried to head her towards the bridge she started to run towards the scrubland in the distance. Afraid of being cheated of his booty,

66

Choran the red-mouthed hurried in pursuit, brandishing a stick and yelling, while Tipane ran alongside him, hurling stones and abuse at the man.

Moon Horn did not like being pursued. She wheeled round and contemplated the matter with lowered head. Then she charged. Choran Woodcutter's shouts of anger changed to cries of alarm. He went scurrying towards the bridge, but Moon Horn was too fast for him and forced him to retreat towards the river bank, which was steep at that point. In his haste Choran did not realize where he was going, until all at once he was treading on nothing. With a wild yell he fell headlong into the river, while the charging Moon Horn dug in her hooves, came to a shambling halt and swerved away.

While Kishkar watched all this, he became aware of a rippling shape moving across the river, and realized that the crocodile was no longer skulking near the rock—it knew there was more hope now of finding its supper elsewhere than by keeping watch on the rock.

This was Kishkar's chance, his only chance. He must take advantage of this distraction and brave the river. He uttered a prayer to the gods, gathered the heavy cloak round his shoulders and plunged in.

While Kishkar struck out towards the opposite shore, the villagers began to hurry across the bridge. The ramshackle structure creaked and groaned, the posts swayed. If they were not careful there would be more than one supper for the crocodile. But perhaps one was enough.

A hideous scream cleft the air. The spectators halted in a startled huddle and pointed wildly. The crocodile had found its supper: the ugly jaws had seized the would-be thief and dragged him under. The opaque water swirled and hid its secret. The pelicans belched indifferently.

Kishkar felt his feet touch bottom. He stood up and waded out, weary but thankful. The cloak was heavy with water and oranges but with water streaming and dripping from his body, he managed to stumble ashore. Dogs barked, men shouted, but the villagers had no stomach for further pursuit.

The relief of his escape from the nightmare of the river sped Kishkar's heels. Though his lungs felt as if they would burst and his legs as if they had been hamstrung, he ran on, eager to find Tipane and Moon Horn, and to put a good distance between himself and the villagers, whose shrill voices were uglier than the wail of jackals on the fringe of the night.

When presently Kishkar found Tipane and Moon Horn waiting hopefully for him under a clump of palm-trees, he still did not dare halt for long.

"We must go on further," he said in a low voice. "Those men may come and look for us in the morning."

"But I am so tired," Tipane pleaded. "And so hungry."

So Kishkar gave him three of the oranges and took one himself. They squatted on the ground and ate them gratefully. They felt revived straight away and it was as if the rich, sweet juice had entered their blood at once, as honey does. Tipane had nearly finished all his before Kishkar had eaten his solitary orange.

"Come," said Kishkar, jumping up. "We must go on."

"I am a little less hungry," Tipane wheedled. "But I am still very tired. . . ."

Kishkar hesitated. His brother's tiredness would have been a good excuse—a good reason, rather—to have found a place to sleep there and then, and he was nearly tempted. But he thought with a shudder of the river and the covetous men who had so nearly stolen Moon Horn.

68

Nothing in the night could be worse than that. So he hoisted Tipane on to his shoulders and urged Moon Horn forward again. He walked with a hand on the buffalo's side, partly for company's sake, but also to prevent himself stumbling from weariness. The night was thick and daunting, full of subtle whisperings and furtive scufflings and lit only by the scribbling of fireflies.

While Tipane dozed astride Kishkar's shoulders, Kishkar trudged on in company with the heifer. He continued his weary way for a long time after he had left behind any paddy-field or plantain grove or other sign of human activity. By now he had come into undulating scrub country, where long stretches of grassland alternated with thickset lantana bushes. In the distance hyenas uttered their maniacal laughter and somewhere there was a crunching of bones.

As Kishkar plodded on, a massive shape loomed up on the horizon, growing steadily larger as he approached. At first he thought it was a group of trees, but now the moon was rising and he saw it was the silhouette of some kind of building. He came to a halt, one hand on Moon Horn's neck, for he was still chary of meeting anyone. Cautiously, sighing a little under his brother's weight, he moved nearer. Against the shimmering sky he could make out a wall . . . a broad flight of steps . . . an archway with graceful arabesque contours through which the moon burned redly.

The building was a temple, but it was a long time since it had heard the sound of worship. The once dignified steps had crumbled, leaving little more than an earth ramp. The carven elephants that supported the walls had not been powerful enough to resist time and the sapping of tree roots. Kishkar was a little afraid, but his aching limbs

69

rebelled at the thought of going any further. He and Tipane and Moon Horn would be safe for the night in the shelter of the ruined temple.

As he laboured up the crumbling steps, holding Tipane firmly, he saw a faint light in the courtyard. It was the flicker of firelight, and he could smell cow-dung burning. Someone else had sought shelter in the ruins. But it was too far from the river for anyone to know what had happened and the fire seemed so friendly that Kishkar walked towards it across the silent courtyard.

An old man was sitting before it, small and shrivelled and clad in a dark robe. Kishkar paused, waiting for him to speak, but the old man continued to squat in silence, leaning forward slightly, as if he could see something of the utmost importance in the smouldering fire: he was deep in contemplation.

Now Moon Horn had scrambled up the derelict steps after Kishkar. She did not hesitate, but uttered a grassy sigh and sank down on the flagstones that were still warm from the day's heat: she had no fear of the old man.

Kishkar wondered whether to announce himself—he did not wish to show disrespect by interrupting the old man's thoughts. But the little fire was so welcoming and the old man so peaceful that Kishkar soon lifted Tipane from his shoulders and set him, murmuring in his sleep, close to the fire. Then, having spread his wet cloak over the ruined wall, Kishkar, too, curled up with an arm round his brother, and neither the whining mosquitoes nor the far-off imprecations of hyenas and jackals could keep him from the blessed refuge of sleep in which even hunger was forgotten.

8 *The Bread of Companionship*

"MAY-AWE! MAY-AWE!" the peacock caterwauled, harsh as the tearing of calico. Aware of its beauty, it displayed its gaudy, ocellated tail as it perched on the ruined wall, so that the early sunlight burnished it as if it were encrusted with gems. The deep turquoise of the peacock's breast shimmered, too, so that it looked like a bird a poet might have created rather than a living creature. "May-awe! May-awe!" it cried again, in a voice ugly as the malediction of a squabbling cat—as if the poet had lapsed into bazaar-talk.

The noise made Kishkar stir in his sleep and try to get rid of the stone that was weighing him down. He dreamt that he was attempting to lift the great round temple stone, but hard though he strove he could not shift it from his chest. He groaned and writhed and suddenly, when the peacock shrieked again, the stone was gone. Tipane sat up, too, his face puckered with sleep, and complained at being disturbed, for he had been using his brother as a pillow and his head had been the temple stone.

For a moment Kishkar looked around him uncomprehendingly at the shattered pillars and the derelict courtyard. A canopy of evergreen asoka trees dangled their tenderly brilliant clusters of scarlet and orange flowers above the place. Their roots pushed up the uneven flagstones or reft the massive walls that were supported by carven elephants which paraded endlessly round, trunk to tail, trunk to tail. Coral creeper with its heart-shaped leaves and pink flowers hung draped over the ornate gateway, like ropes being used to dismantle it. Moonbeam flowers shone in at the unglazed window slots of the shrines.

On the sun-warmed steps, little spotted doves stretched their wings luxuriously. Pert ground squirrels chattered irreverently among the twining, elaborate figures of Hindu gods and goddesses with many heads and more arms. A mongoose scampered out from exploring one of the shrines for rats. In a stone-bordered pool beyond the courtyard, dainty grey cranes stalked among the water-lilies, hunting for frogs.

It seemed as if nature were intent on showing how easily she could usurp this temple over which many generations of craftsmen had toiled.

Kishkar's wonderment was interrupted by a tugging hand.

"When shall we eat?" Tipane asked urgently.

"Where is Moon Horn?" Kishkar came to his wits. He sprang to his feet and anxiously surveyed the temple. He uttered a cry of dismay as he caught sight of a huge black bull lying on a plinth at the far end of the courtyard. But then he realized it was a sacred idol made of stone and would do Moon Horn no harm. To his relief he saw that Moon Horn had gone down from the temple and was grazing on the scrawny grassland which alternated with thickets of lantana scrub.

As he watched the heifer, he became aware that the old man in the dark yellow robe was still squatting tranquilly by the ashes of the fire. It was as if he had not moved all night. But now he was no longer deep in meditation: instead he gazed benignly at Kishkar and Tipane, nodding his grizzled head and smiling without cease. It was not perhaps so much that he smiled as that a friendly radiance glowed from him, like warmth from a fire even when no flames are evident.

Kishkar saw that the stranger was a holy man. He could tell from the colour of his robe, and from the ash marks on his forehead and arms, and the necklace of rudrashka seeds, large as nutmegs, round the wrinkled neck. He was a Jangama of the sect of Siva and, though Kishkar was not a Hindu, he knew that any holy man deserved respect. He also knew that a man of any other sect might not have tolerated him and Tipane at his fireside. Hurriedly he made namasta at the old man and Tipane did so too without waiting to get up.

"Salaam, holy man," Kishkar said, bowing several times. "I ask pardon for trespassing at your fire. I would have asked your permission last night, but I was afraid to disturb your thoughts and we were tired. . . ."

"It is I who should ask pardon," the old man smiled. "For a fire without a cooking-pot is only half a fire."

"What does he mean?" Tipane whispered at Kishkar's elbow. "That he hasn't any food?"

"Indeed, your buffalo is the only fortunate one among us," the Jangama continued, "for she at least can crop the grass, whereas you and I, it seems, can only chew the cud of thought."

"That is Moon Horn, my heifer," said Kishkar, straightening his back. Moon Horn was sacred among the buffaloes of the Blue Hills, descended from a celestial line, and Kishkar felt this put him nearly on equal terms with a holy man.

"You have travelled far? I think you are not from these parts?"

73

"We have come a great distance," ventured Tipane, pouting. He moved nearer to the Jangama. "Yesterday we ate only oranges and coconut milk. I am very hungry."

"We come from the Blue Hills," Kishkar began to explain, lowering his face and staring at the smouldering remnants of the fire. He felt embarrassed at telling the Jangama where they came from, for despite their mildness the old man's eyes had a penetrating quality.

"Did you need proof that your home was good?" the old man asked gently. "Was your Moon Horn dissatisfied with her pasture that she needed to taste this grass which is as cropped as a priest's head?"

"I wasn't dissatisfied with my home," Tipane declared stoutly. His chin drooped a little and he blinked his eyes, but he knew he must be loyal to his brother.

"I left the Blue Hills because Moon Horn was in peril," Kishkar muttered, dropping down on his haunches. Slowly at the outset, but with growing ease, for he trusted this amiable old man, he explained what had happened. It comforted him to have someone with whom he could talk and it made him feel less lonely. Attentively the Jangama listened, leaning forward slightly. Tipane had moved close to him now and the old man put out an arm to draw him down to his side.

"It is sad that someone so young should leave his home," the Jangama remarked presently, when at last Kishkar had recounted everything to do with the People of the Buffalo. "One's own hearth and the love that surrounds it is the only true warmth. There are greater heats than this. For example, the heat of the sun is life-giving but also terrible." He raised a hand at the fierce orb that was already dispersing the freshness of the early morning, in which for a brief moment everything seemed to have been created anew.

74

"There is the heat of great flames, but, like anger, they can be all-consuming. But the warmth of one's home is the only constant warmth, for although men may be too poor even to burn wood on their hearth, the warmth in their hearts will sustain them and their families."

"When the fire on our hearth falls low," said Tipane, twisting round to gaze up at the walnut-coloured, walnut-wrinkled face of the Jangama, "our mother blows on it through a bamboo tube to put life in it."

"But wasn't it unjust that this fat white sahib who stole our sacred Buffalo Bell should have caused our misfortune?" Kishkar demanded. He was somewhat aggrieved that the Jangama had not evinced more sympathy. "But for that I would have been the dairy-priest's acolyte, next to him in honour . . . ."

"Honour is an empty husk unless it is merited," said the Jangama, "and perhaps injustice is the scourge that toughens our skins. The truth is often concealed from us. Men only value diamonds and rubies because they have to be sought at great cost and labour in the bowels of the earth. Maybe the truth will be vouchsafed you in the course of your exile."

Kishkar did not particularly like all this, for it seemed akin to a reproach, but he nodded respectfully, feeling that he must show agreement with one so venerable. The truth of his case seemed all too evident to him; his face grew sullen as he thought of his misfortunes, and his heart contracted with homesickness.

"Have you travelled far, holy man?" he asked presently, while Tipane fingered the old man's necklace.

"I seek the truth also," the Jangama replied quietly. "Where I shall find it, I do not know. I came here to this place to contemplate before the Bull of Munjara, the

75

favoured of Siva. But the end of my journey will be at
Benares, where I shall bathe in the Ganges, the holy river."

"But that is far away!" Kishkar stared. He had heard of
the Ganges as if it were a legend. "More miles away than
there are days in a man's life, I would say. Many months'
journey."

His own wanderings seemed insignificant in comparison
with the task this frail old man had set himself.

"Many moons away," the Jangama nodded, smiling.
"Perhaps it will not be granted me to reach my goal. But
perhaps I shall acquire a little virtue on the way."

"But where will you get food for such a journey?"
Tipane asked, deeply disturbed but practical.

"The gods will provide, little friend. They will
whisper to people and make them open their hearts." As
the old man spoke he drew aside a corner of his yellow
robe and indicated his wooden begging-bowl. "Will
you and your brother accompany me on my journey, and
we will eat the bread of companionship together?"

"The bread of companionship?" echoed Tipane. The
suggestion of food of any kind made him pass a regretful
hand over his belly.

"Perhaps time and distance will heal your hurts and help
you to forget your home," the Jangama added, with a
sly look for Kishkar's benefit. Kishkar stared at the old man
in sudden horror as he had a vision of himself and Tipane
and Moon Horn getting further and further away from the
Blue Hills. He had never really considered before now
where he was going. He had only been concerned with
the need to escape and to safeguard Moon Horn.

"I must think," he said, jumping suddenly to his feet, so
that the little doves rose with a clatter of wings and the
peacock went sailing down towards the lantana bushes.

He walked over to the temple wall and gazed abstractedly into the distance. As he did so, it was as if a knife had been plunged into his heart. For there, far away and dim on the horizon, beyond all those weary miles he had trudged, lay the outline of the Blue Hills. . . .

He could not bear it. He turned his back abruptly and, leaping down the broken steps, went running out into the grassland to look for Moon Horn.

When he had gone a short way among the lantanas he came across the buffalo heifer, who had finished her grazing, such as it was, and was lying sedately in the shade chewing the cud, her moist, mild eyes staring drowsily into complacent nothingness. Round her a pair of bush-chats flitted, darting after the insects that pestered her and uttering an appreciative chorus of *chek, chek, chek*. Blurred by the heat haze that fluttered in the distance of the grass-land, a little herd of blackbuck antelopes ranged uneasily.

Presently the bushchats flew off and Moon Horn scrambled to her feet, shaking her horns. Kishkar saw a dog-like animal come humpling past. It was all grinning jaw and head and its spotted hind-quarters sloped away as if it were crippled.

Kishkar searched for a weapon, for the hyena's calculating eyes glowed as they confirmed what his nostrils had suspected. In his tucked-up, cringing way he circled round, blunt ears cocked, snout wavering as he enjoyed the scent of the buffalo. It was odd coming across a buffalo and a human being out here in the scrub. Maybe there was something wrong . . . the buffalo was sick perhaps and it would be possible to rush in and hamstring it.

While Moon Horn shambled round breathing alarm and Kishkar kept watch, the hyena loped out of sight behind them; he always preferred to work from behind.

77

As he skulked through the scented lantana he uttered his sneering laugh. That same poet had composed some lines that didn't scan when he thought up the laugh of the hyena and the scream of the peacock!

The hyena knew well the nerve-racking effect of his hideous guffaw. It was a sound policy to scare one's victims, for then they acted rashly.

But the hyena could not concentrate: something was distracting him. He lifted his muzzle again to quest the flaccid air, limp with dust and pollen and heat, and with the powerful scent of the lantanas.

Kishkar, too, was aware that something untoward was happening in the distance. Out in the greasy waves of heat that dithered up from the earth, the blackbuck were picking their way more hurriedly. Until they moved they had looked like half animals for their dark upper parts merged in the patchwork of the scrub, while their white bellies and white-striped legs were as apparent as fresh paint. They pricked their ears, raised their pronged heads and tip-toed on. Then a sudden panic seized them. and like leaves sent scurrying by the wind they went racing off, sometimes bounding in the air, sometimes obscured by bush or tree. Then curiosity got the better of them and they halted to gaze back in the direction from which they had run.

From far away, growing closer all the time, came a rumbling, grinding noise, as of some strange unworldly creature labouring and lurching nearer. Kishkar poised uneasily, looking with narrowed eyes across the undulating, burnt-up grassland. The droning noise grew steadily louder and he was minded to run back to the temple and warn the Jangama. But, like the blackbuck, he was curious.

78

Now the sunlight glinted and flashed like the notes of a bugle on glass and metal. Into view came a motor-car, brilliantly polished, its tall bonnet and enormous brass headlights like some grotesque mask.

Before long the motor-car slowed down and came to a halt in the shade of some flame-of-the-forest trees. Out of it leapt men in turbans and drill coats and tight white trousers. Kishkar saw that one of them was leading a large beast on a leash. It had a kind of hood over its head, while its coat, tawny as sand, was marked with spots like black flowers. Its legs were long, its waist was slim and it moved at the side of its attendant with a tense yet supple grace.

9 *The Royal Hunt*

KISHKAR drew back into cover and glanced anxiously at Moon Horn, who was always his main concern. But he need not have worried. The men were talking quietly and were clearly interested in the blackbuck, which were moving on again nervously, a few hundred paces away.

The youngest of the band of hunters, a youth in a blue turban and jodhpurs, seemed to be the leader. The attendant who had led the cheetah out of the car took the hood from its head and unslipped the leash from its collar. Its small, neat head alert, the cheetah went padding eagerly forward. It needed no bidding: it knew what was expected of it. Yet even now the antelopes felt secure in the distance and their own fleetness. An old buck remained behind to shake his fine horns as if in derision. But that was foolish, thought Kishkar, for now he recognized the menace in the cheetah's appearance.

As smoothly as water flowing over rocks, the cheetah bounded on, the sinews of swiftness rippling beneath its flowered pelt. The blackbuck were truly alarmed now. They broke into a trot, sending up a spurt of dust. The cheetah appeared to make no great effort, shoulders and haunches and limbs worked in such velvet unison, yet the distance between it and the herd closed perceptibly. The blackbuck raced on at top speed, aware that death would strike the laggard.

80

Meanwhile, the young man and his companions had jumped into the car. The vehicle went grinding and bouncing across the grassland. Gears crashed like the teeth of a hungry beast. At headlong speed, trumpeting from its exhaust, the motor-car thundered on, drawing a veil of dust behind it. At the steering-wheel the blue-turbanned young man smiled as he glanced at the speedo-meter needle quivering round the dial. Forty miles an hour . . . forty-five . . . the car lurched on, the occupants shouted in mingled triumph and alarm and clung on to their turbans . . . fifty . . . sixty . . . . Yet even at this speed the man-made machine could not outpace the hunting-leopard, this creature of muscle and sinew, that went streaking and pistoning across the sun-baked ground.

Awed yet elated by the spectacle of the chase, Kishkar forgot all caution and ran through the lantanas, hoping to see the end of it. But though he ran till the blood pounded in his temples, he could not keep up.

Swift as the chase was, or because it was so swift, it did not last long. On delicate legs the blackbuck bounded, keen as the wind, heads high in panic, but they could not hope to elude the slim, scudding, tawny shape that closed in behind them. Swifter than a saluki, swifter than many a bird, the cheetah held on relentlessly, swift as doom! And to that one antelope which had rashly lingered, it was doom itself.

The speed of the cheetah bore the blackbuck down in a violent swirling thud as it sprang. The noise of the impact was like the driving of a giant fist into the palm of a giant hand. In a dusty explosion the two animals crashed head-long, slithered and heaved in a terrible embrace. Then both lay still, the buck in death, the cheetah with its fangs biting into the neck-cord of its victim.

Behind them the motor-car drove up. Brakes squealed, doors slammed, and the hunters leapt out, shouting triumphantly. The cheetah had done the killing, but the men took the glory of it to themselves. One of them ran towards the cheetah. A knife glittered in one hand, in the other he held a wooden bowl with a handle. Quickly, expertly, he slit the blackbuck's throat and caught the blood in the bowl. He offered the blood to the cheetah to drink, and only then did the cheetah release its hold.

From afar Kishkar watched much of this, while the young man—who was surely a prince or rajah's son, judging by his dress and demeanour—praised the cheetah. He fondled and patted it as if it were a dog, and the cheetah pressed against him as tamely as a dog, its gold-studded collar glittering in the sun. Kishkar watched, still breathing hard, not only from the running but because there had been something vastly beautiful, yet terrible, in the speed and power of the cheetah.

While he watched, he heard the noise of another machine approaching. It was coming nearer to him than the first car and he was on the point of running away: but it was too late. The second motor-car came fast across the dusty plain and Kishkar crouched down in a lantana bush, not daring to cry out even when the thorns pricked him. He closed his eyes in fear at the clattering noise, expecting this metal monster to charge down on him. But the roar of the engine suddenly diminished and when he opened his eyes again he saw that the car had swerved away and was driving towards the first vehicle. It drew up alongside, and there stepped from it an enormously fat man in whose turban a jewel glittered like a huge and watchful eye. He was obviously an eminent personage, a rajah most likely, for he was attended by a servant bearing a tasselled sunshade. The young man, who was no doubt his son, greeted him deferentially, brushing a hand across his heart, lips and forehead in salute; they were evidently Moslems.

Rugs were spread on the ground in the shade of a tulip tree, whose crimson bell flowers were beginning to burst, and the cheetah was led before the rajah for his praise. Then the servants carried wicker hampers from the motor-cars and a feast was prepared for the refreshment of the rajah and the prince. At least, to the famished Kishkar it seemed a feast, so many things were laid. But to the obese rajah it was merely a picnic, a morning snack to sustain him in his task of carrying round such a great mass of flesh during the day.

For a considerable time the rajah and his son and their sirdars feasted, sitting cross-legged on the rugs, while two servants attended to their wants. Kishkar could hear the shrill, gay chatter of conversation. He was curious to see more of these princely hunters who followed the chase in motor-cars, so he skulked cautiously from bush to bush.

When the picnic had been proceeding for some time and the rajah was licking his fingers, a man came running towards the group of hunters and salaamed breathlessly. Kishkar saw that it was the attendant who had been in charge of the cheetah. He pointed emphatically into the scrub and had apparently brought news of fresh game. The young prince sprang to his feet and led the cheetah into the first car, while the rajah shouted in his shrill voice at the servants, telling them to help him up. Then both cars drove off in a swirl of dust to continue the hunt, the servants standing on the running-board and clinging to the side of the rajah's machine.

For some time afterwards, while the sound of the engines faded, Kishkar hung about near the picnic site. Without quite realizing it, he drew closer to the place where the rajah's party had been feasting. Many of the items had been left, scarcely touched, and in his present hungry state it seemed strange to him that men should abandon such good food. The sight of it was almost painful to him. He put a hand to his belly as if to silence its nagging talk, then, with a quick look round to make certain he was not being watched, he darted in and started to feed. His hunger quickly overcame his hesitation and he stuffed into his mouth anything that came to hand, chappattis, sickly sweetmeats shaped into little golden curlicues, balls of rice and saffron, spicy mysteries, anything.

It was only after gulping many mouthfuls that he stopped. Even then it was not because he had finished, but because he had thought of the Jangama and Tipane. His face darkened with shame that he had forgotten them in his greed. Hastily he surveyed the remains of the feast, then snatched up various little plantains, a few mangoes and a handful of chappattis. Clutching them to his chest, he went scuttling furtively away. The chappattis were somewhat dry and inclined to crumble, but that could not be helped.

Once out of sight of the tulip tree, he slowed to a walk, for it was difficult to carry the pile of food. The chappattis and the rice balls were so good he didn't want to spoil them. As he approached the temple Tipane came running towards him and halted in astonishment at the sight of the food.

"Where have you been? Moon Horn returned by herself and I was afraid . . . Is it real?" he cried, running here and there round Kishkar in order to get a better view of the good things in his brother's arms. "Is it magic?"

"Wait!" smiled Kishkar, hurrying on up the flight of steps, eager to show the Jangama what he had brought.

"See, holy man!" he burst out as he reached the courtyard. "The gods have whispered and made men open-hearted, as you said!"

Whether such open-heartedness was an attribute of the fat rajah was a questionable point, but the effect was the same.

"Rather have the gods shouted," remarked the Jangama drily as he surveyed the pile of food that Kishkar set before him.

"We will eat together," declared Tipane, almost tripping over himself in his eagerness to get a place at the feast.

Kishkar squatted nearby, watching with approval while the old man and his brother fed under the asoka trees. He had violated the table of a great rajah, a crime for which he would assuredly have been beaten with lathis had he been caught. But he was rewarded by the sight of the Jangama and Tipane eating so heartily. The juice of mangoes trickled down their chins, the crumbs of chappattis spattered their chests. Every now and then the two exchanged appreciative glances. The Jangama was in no way concerned about where Kishkar had acquired the food. He received it as evidence of the bounty of the gods.

Kishkar felt a kind of purring warmth within him from the good food. He hoped Moon Horn had eaten her fill, too, and saw that she was drinking at the temple pool, no doubt to wash down the red dust with which her scrawny pasture was coated. More dust than sap seemed to be her lot at present.

The old man and the small boy happily ate their way through the rajah's unwitting bounty. Both of them were breathing heavily by now and between times they grunted or nodded at each other.

Kishkar surveyed the diminishing feast and decided that

he must act for the morrow. He picked up the Jangama's begging-bowl and hurried from the ruined temple: he would return to the picnic place for a refill. The banqueters scarcely noticed his departure.

"These sweetmeats are pleasant as a generous thought," murmured the holy man, helping himself to an elaborate curlicue that had been made with such care in the royal kitchens.

"Truly," agreed Tipane, with a portentousness beyond his years, "truly the bread of companionship is delicious."

The profundity of his statement was emphasized rather than spoilt by the eloquent belch that shook him as he spoke.

10 *Fear in the Night*

As the sun drummed higher in the incandescent sky, a heavy calm settled upon the ruined temple. The neat little spotted doves ceased their croodling in the asoka trees. The ground squirrels took themselves off into the shelter of niches and holes, making certain that no snakes were lurking there. Even the coppersmith bird ceased for a while to beat out his monotonous refrain—and when the coppersmith is mute it is hot indeed.

It was not only the heat that affected the Jangama and Tipane: both the old man and the small boy had been silenced just as much by their meal. It was a long time since either of them had eaten their fill, and certainly neither had ever before enjoyed such sumptuous fare.

The holy man had announced his intention of worshipping before the Black Bull of Munjara that lay eternally on guard in the courtyard. He recited many prayers and made various little offerings, but it was noticeable that to do so he chose the coolest spot, where the coral creeper formed a pleasant bower, and the carved stone elephants round the plinth of the inner building provided a snug backrest—should he need it. With folded hands he squatted tailor-fashion, part-covered by the dark robe that was so yellow as to be almost red. He nodded more frequently than ever: apparently he could meditate better with closed eyes.

Tipane lay not far away, his face gleaming both with sweat and the smeared testimony of his feast. He slept tucked against the gently heaving flank of Moon Horn who was drowsily chewing the cud. She, too, had enjoyed her best meal for several days, simply because there had been plenty of time. Though the grass in the scrubland among the pungent lantana bushes was meagre and dusty, she had found some lush tid-bits growing round the edge of the temple pool. Now her tail flicked idly in response to the attentions of various insects, and Tipane benefited also from its motion as it passed immediately above his head without hitting him.

Only Kishkar was wide awake. He was gratified to see Tipane and Moon Horn well fed; glad, too, that they were able to spend the day resting instead of trudging on through strange and often hostile countryside. It was the first time since they had fled from the Blue Hills that they had been able to rest properly. The nights had been too uneasy, the days too anxious. But here in the abandoned temple they would be safe for a while. There were no envious villagers to shout abuse at him or to try to steal Moon Horn, while the friendly presence of the old Jangama was comforting after the days of loneliness and worry.

Even so, Kishkar's mood of relief at this temporary peace was disturbed by that long rolling horizon of the Blue Hills framed in the evergreen branches of the asoka tree beneath which he was sitting. He felt stifled with homesickness and his tears blurred the outline of the hills so that they became a mere smudge. He wondered if the people who had once worshipped at this temple had suffered some terrible disaster in the same way as the People of the Buffalo had with the theft of the sacred Buffalo Bell? Had their fortunes declined from then onwards and their temple been deserted and fallen in ruins? Would the same fate befall the People?

Kishkar's heart was heavy as he turned away. He could not bear to gaze at the Blue Hills any longer. He looked at the Jangama drowsing in front of the stone bull. He looked at his brother sleeping with his head on one arm. He looked at Moon Horn placidly chewing. Nobody else seemed to have any problems. Only Kishkar!

As Kishkar sat thinking this, Moon Horn turned her head and gazed trustingly at him out of her long-lashed, dew-moist eyes. It was as if she understood his troubles and dumbly showed her sympathy and gratitude. Kishkar nodded slowly. At least he had done right in saving Moon Horn. Who could tell what even greater disaster might have struck the People if the little heifer, survivor of a sacred line, had perished unnecessarily at the death stone?

Kishkar's meditations were presently interrupted by a strange murmur that drifted across the hazy scrubland. An intent look came into his eyes. He rose to one knee and listened, then he stood up and walked to the temple steps. A column of dust was moving across the landscape. The murmur grew to a grumbling drone. It could mean only one thing: the royal hunters were returning. Kishkar was suddenly worried. Could it be because of him?

One of the cars had halted near the picnic site again and some of the men descended. They seemed to be searching for something, for they began to scour the neighbourhood, hurrying to and fro and calling to each other. They argued loudly. Some of them pointed towards the temple, others gestured in disagreement and pointed back into the scrub. They stooped and were apparently examining tracks on the ground. Kishkar hoped they would not find his foot-prints.

Then the rajah stood up in the car and screamed angrily at the hunters. Kishkar had never heard a person sound so angry, not even Paramajoti when the Buffalo Bell was stolen. Kishkar could not help trembling. He remembered only too vividly the previous evening's encounter when a few oranges had cost him so dear. Assuredly he would not like to fall foul of that rajah in his present mood. Yet surely a great man like that would not bother his head over a few scraps of food which the jackals might have filched?

Before long the other motor-car drove up. The young prince jumped out and ran across to his father. Kishkar could tell that the prince was upset, too, not, it seemed, because of the rajah's anger, but because something untoward had happened.

For a while the commotion continued and Kishkar heard a babble of shrill voices and the shriek of a man being beaten. It was all most disturbing. Kishkar dreaded that the men might take it into their heads to visit the temple, and he was considerably relieved when the motor-cars drove off again in a flurry of dust.

But they returned—not once but several times, though mainly at a distance. They appeared and reappeared through the scrub and along the dried up water-courses. It was as if they had lost their way or were searching for something.

Hidden behind the tumbledown wall of the temple, Kishkar witnessed all this in considerable apprehension. He clutched a shoulder with his hand, as if in anticipation of the blows he might receive from the rajah's servants.

Only when the sun had foundered in a sea of livid colour beyond the dusty landscape and nightjars were beginning to glide on mothlike wings round the temple, did the motor-cars go away, bumping and complaining as they churned across the rough ground, their headlights cutting swordlike slashes in the distance as night fell. Only then did Kishkar relax.

He slept heavily, but he had bad dreams, perhaps because he had eaten too much. Certainly his belly troubled him. He muttered in his sleep and clutched the butter-smelling cloak for protection. He tossed and turned on the hard stones of the courtyard and his face glistened with sweat. He was being pursued. He ran this way and that, trying to escape. He put up a hand to ward off the danger and sharp claws sank cruelly into his flesh. With a cry he turned, only to find a bright light gleaming in his eyes. It must be one of the motor-cars that had searched him out with its headlights shining straight at him, pinning him down as surely as a spear. Instantly he awoke and shielded his eyes from the brilliant light. But it was the moon that shone upon him and the pain in his arm was from a thorn that had scratched him, not the claws of some ravening beast.

It had been a disturbing dream and Kishkar did not feel confident enough to settle down to sleep again. Out in the scrub the hyenas and the jackals were cracking their maniac jokes. What strange, unseen life went on out there under cover of darkness, where eyeballs bulged and ears strained and tails twitched?

Kishkar wished the little cow-dung fire was still burning, for dawn was not far off and a dank chill made him draw the cloak tightly about him as he sat there with hands round knees, eyeing the great stone bull towering over the courtyard and thinking how clumsy it looked in comparison with Moon Horn. Not far away the Jangama snored serenely, but Tipane was whimpering in his sleep and had rolled away from Moon Horn's side.

91

Kishkar went over to his brother and, sitting down, wrapped them both in the cloak. But Tipane awoke and threw it off feverishly.

"I'm so thirsty," he muttered, wriggling his shoulders.

"Go to sleep again," Kishkar urged, in a low voice. You always spoke softly at night; you never knew who or what might be listening. "It will soon be morning."

"But my mouth is on fire," Tipane complained, sitting up. "I feel as if I'd swallowed live coals."

"We can't go now," Kishkar answered. The temple pool was not far away but he did not fancy the idea of venturing down there at night, even though the moon was still casting its dreamlike splendour over everything. But Tipane was so restless and insistent that in the end he had to give in.

Reluctantly Kishkar took Tipane by the hand and led him across the courtyard that was patterned with phalanxes of shadows and gashes of light. Here and there among the lantana thickets furtive eyes smouldered where the jackals cringed, intrigued by the occupants of the temple that was usually deserted. They wailed constantly, urging each other to go closer, but none of them dared.

As the boys went towards the pool a different, shuffling sound made Kishkar halt. He knew it was not a jackal.

"Come, I must drink," begged Tipane, tugging him on.

"Hush! Can't you hear?" whispered Kishkar.

Kishkar was alarmed by the strange sound: it was as if something were crawling furtively, stalking them, lurking in the shadows. But he tried to suppress his fear because of Tipane. Together the brothers waited, alert, tense, their eyes huge in the lingering moonlight.

Kishkar walked on a few paces, Tipane's hand clammy in his. Step by step they made their way among the jigsaw puzzle of shadows. The asoka leaves rustled, the nightjars uttered cries that resembled the skimming of stones across ice, a hyena chuckled throatily, scuffled and snarled. It was not that, either. The sound Kishkar had heard was close, horribly close. He wanted to run, but he knew he must discover what was happening down there beyond the curtain of shadows. It might be some creature that had come to threaten Moon Horn.

Now Tipane was no longer tugging Kishkar on. He had forgotten his thirst and was pulling his brother the other way again, but Kishkar shook him off and walked down the steps to the temple pool, where the frogs sat on their lily-pad platforms and croaked longingly of the monsoon rains that were still so many weeks off.

In mingled fear and determination, Kishkar advanced with hurried breath and tingling nerves, ready for he knew not what peril. As he emerged from the shadows he saw something move slowly, forebodingly, along the flagstones that bordered the pool. It was a large, lank beast skulking towards the glimmering water.

Catching his breath, Kishkar stood poised for flight. The beast by the pool halted, too, crouching ready to spring. In the moonlight a pair of ruby eyes stared up at Kishkar, and Kishkar returning the gaze could plainly see a spotted, tawny, menacing form.

It was the cheetah.

11 *God's Flower*

"WILL it eat us and leave our bones for the jackals?" Tipane whispered. "We must run!"

"It would overtake you in one stride," Kishkar answered, hoarsely. "I have seen. It is faster than the wind."

"Perhaps it has come to seize Moon Horn," Tipane muttered.

For a long time the two brothers waited, not daring to move for fear the cheetah might attack them. The animal continued to crouch a few paces away, gazing at them out of its sombre eyes.

Now the moon slid away behind the bush and for a while all was ugly blackness, save for the lingering stars and the shifting ring of green eye-specks where the jackals patrolled. Kishkar was sure the cheetah was drawing stealthily closer. He could hear the strange, shuffling, rattling noise again . . . as well as the thumping of his own heart, and the chattering of Tipane's teeth, that was louder than the cry of the chik-chak lizards.

It seemed many years before the last stars were snuffed out, and by then Kishkar's limbs were shaking with the tension. His eyeballs hurt as he stared at the dark shape of the cheetah, endeavouring to make out whether it was moving nearer; and when presently the first touch of dawn began to end the siege of darkness, Kishkar saw that the cheetah had indeed come closer. It appeared to hesitate

94

as if it, too, were afraid. Kishkar noticed that it limped, and that whenever it moved the strange dragging sound occurred.

"It's hurt!" he muttered, frowning, for a wounded beast could be even more dangerous than one that was not. Yet he was beginning to feel that the cheetah had no evil intent. It seemed to be approaching in an almost pleading way.

"It has something round its hind leg!" hissed Tipane, pointing. In his curiosity his fear was evaporating.

"Yes," Kishkar agreed, watching intently as the cheetah limped forward again uncertainly. "It has been caught in a trap."

From the cheetah's leg trailed a length of wire, at the end of which was a heavy, pointed, wooden stake: this was the explanation of the unnerving sound. This, too, was the explanation of why the royal hunters had kept coming and going so oddly: they had been searching for the trapped cheetah.

By now the wounded cheetah had approached to within hand's reach of Kishkar. Now that he knew the reason for its behaviour it no longer seemed that the animal glared up at him menacingly. Rather, its expression was one of trust, as if it were confident that it had found friends who would help it. Kishkar knew that he must conquer his fear and do what he could for this graceful creature whose awesome power he had witnessed on the previous day.

The wire snare had bitten into the upper part of the cheetah's leg, tearing the smooth white inner thigh and leaving an ugly jagged furrow. Some peasant had set a trap for a wild pig that was raiding his crops, maybe, and the cheetah had passed that way. It was fortunate the cheetah had not put its neck in the snare or by now it would be glassy-eyed in the agony of strangulation.

Kishkar hesitated as he considered how to set about removing the wire, which was embedded in the flesh. Clearly it was causing the cheetah a great deal of pain, for the animal panted in distress, but it would hurt even more as he loosened the wire.

"It has very powerful claws," Tipane whispered discouragingly, squatting nearby, torn between fascination and alarm. "And its fangs are sharp and hungry-looking!"

"Be silent!" said Kishkar, impatiently. "This beast has come to us for help. He is used to the company of men. He trusts in us to help him."

As he spoke these words Kishkar lost his fear, encouraged by the truth of his own thoughts. He felt suddenly glad at the chance of helping the cheetah, for he was beginning to appreciate the meaning of being alone and in trouble.

"He is covered in flowers," murmured Tipane, emboldened by his brother's attitude. He stretched out a timid hand to touch the cheetah's flank but snatched it away again immediately as if he had burnt himself. "I will tell the holy man," he said, jumping up and running into the temple courtyard, where the spotted doves went skimming away, their delicate wings shot through by the resplendent morning light that flooded over the land.

Meanwhile, certain that Kishkar was going to help, the cheetah had stretched out on the flagstones. It raised its neat head and looked up, as if mutely begging him to hurry. The wire snare was hurting. Kishkar nodded and, kneeling down, set about the task. He needed steady fingers. He could feel the hot throbbing of the cheetah's blood above the wound, and the chill of the limb below the ligature.

Kishkar's face was shadowed with a frown. He would have screamed if he had suffered as the cheetah must be suffering. Yet the creature lay there trustingly, panting a little, its pale amber flank heaving rhythmically, framed in the dark bars of Kishkar's glistening arms.

Quickly now, for it had to be done, Kishkar picked at the wire with his finger-tips in order not to pull at the wounded flesh. He worked delicately as a bazaar watchmender to avoid causing more pain, but even so the cheetah trembled, its claws gripped convulsively, the tip of its tail switched faintly.

Then Kishkar felt the wire come away. Eagerly he worked the noose open and drew it carefully from the tortured limb. At once the cheetah bent round lissomly began to rasp with its tongue at the wound. Kishkar took hold of the snare and the stake and with a cry of disgust flung them from him.

"She sings," said the Jangama, who, unbeknown to Kishkar, had been squatting close by. "The cheetah tells of her gratitude to you."

Kishkar smiled. For indeed, the cheetah was purring and Kishkar felt a deep satisfaction at having helped this beautiful yet terrible creature, which the gods had made swifter than any other.

"But the wound is deep," he murmured presently, watching as the cheetah licked and licked. He waved a hand to drive away the flies that were already gathering.

"She applies the medicine of her tongue," Tipane remarked, this time boldly laying a hand on the cheetah's collar, on which, though neither the Jangama nor the boys could read it, was inscribed the name of Hansia.

"I have a medicine to cure that wound and any other," said the Jangama, fumbling in the folds of his robe. He

97

drew out a few stems of a plant with little flowers like daisies and leaves that were fleshy and serrated at the edges. "God's Flower, this plant is called. Take and rub the leaves between your fingers and let the juice fall on the wound."

"This is good medicine?" Kishkar asked, wonderingly, as he took the limp plant.

"Assuredly," the Jangama nodded. "I have healed many sores and wounds with that. I carry it with me always. It grows in the jungle. When this is used I will seek more."

Smelling the pungent scent as he crushed the leaves between his fingers, Kishkar gently pushed Hansia's head away so that he could apply the Jangama's medicine. Obediently the cheetah lay on its side again, trusting Kishkar. Carefully the boy made certain that the healing juice seeped into the raw furrow and while he knelt there Hansia started to purr again as if she had a little machine in her throat.

At length the cheetah stood up and limped down to the pool. She crouched at the edge and began to drink urgently, deeply. Kishkar thought that now Hansia would depart, but presently, when the boys and the old man sat under the asoka tree breaking their fast on the remnants of the rajah's picnic, the cheetah entered the court-yard and sociably lay down in front of them. Once or twice it raised its head as if interested in seeing them eat.

"She is envious that we are feeding," mumbled Tipane, the juice of a paw-paw trickling down his chin.

"She must be hungry," Kishkar said, pausing to survey Hansia. "She hasn't been able to hunt because of her wound."

"If she will eat fruit, there's plenty," said Tipane, hope-

98

fully proffering a few grapes. The cheetah started to purr again, but turned her whiskered face away from Tipane's hand.

"Flesh," said the Jangama, pausing to spit out a troublesome piece of peel, "flesh is the only food such a creature likes."

The cheetah stood up and limped towards the temple steps where she stood staring out alertly across the scrubland. Tipane went to Hansia's side to discover what she was so interested in. His news was alarming.

"Moon Horn is grazing down there," he cried to Kishkar. "The hunting-leopard is watching very hungrily, it seems to me."

"I must find food for her," Kishkar replied. He had feared all along that the cheetah's coming might mean danger for Moon Horn. Even if they left the temple the cheetah might follow them. But how could he satisfy her hunger and turn her attention from the buffalo heifer? He was no hunter, for the People of the Buffalo killed only when they unlocked the door of the Shades for those who had died.

Then he thought of the blackbuck. The cheetah had killed one, possibly two. He knew the rajah's men had not bothered about the first carcase: the hunt had not been for food, but wantonly for sport. Once the blackbuck had been struck down its purpose had been fulfilled. Only the hyenas and the jackals had benefited. They had screamed and jeered their thanks all night and now the vultures wheeled overhead out there in the distance, hoping for a few remnants. If he hurried he might be able to retrieve some morsel to distract the cheetah.

"I am going to find meat for the hunting-leopard," he said.

"Make haste then," counselled Tipane. "This beast with the flowers has a keen look."

"You must borrow the holy man's staff and guard Moon Horn," Kishkar ordered. "I shall not be long."

Already the magic light of the new morning had been adulterated by a blast of dusty heat, as if some giant oven door had been thrown open. Nevertheless, Kishkar went at a steady trot out into the stifling plain. He must lose no time, for truly he was concerned for Moon Horn. It was an undeniable fact that the cheetah lived on flesh and blood and, even in its wounded state, would find the buffalo heifer an easy prey.

Kishkar had no difficulty in locating the remains of the blackbuck. He remembered exactly where he had seen it struck down by the cheetah; besides, he could hear animals squabbling over the remains, and as he loped on he saw yet another Pharaoh's chicken wheel round on wings that were more majestic than its appetite, and flutter down to join the throng.

As he approached the place, he slowed to a walk and presently paused to survey the situation. Two jackals and a hyena were crunching bones not far away, while several vultures sidled nearer to snatch what they could. Little remained but the handsome horns and tattered ribs of the once graceful creature that had bounded so nimbly across the face of the earth.

Kishkar broke a branch from a dead tree that elephants had pushed over at some time. He picked up a stone, too. The offal-mongers paused to look warily at the boy. The jackals whimpered complainingly as if to excuse themselves. The hyena laughed savagely and circled round to see what it all meant.

Kishkar moved a little nearer the pitiful carcase and

sized it up. The most promising remnant was part of a haunch, torn and bloody. It disgusted Kishkar to think of what he was going to do, but for Moon Horn's sake he must defile himself.

The Pharaoh's chickens, with their ugly, yellow, naked heads and soiled white plumage, took advantage of the diversion to waddle nearer with their high-stepping gait. One of them hopped in grotesquely and snatched a gobbet of flesh. At once the hyena rounded on it, snarling resentfully. In a thrashing of wings the vultures jostled out of the way while the hyena lunged at them.

This was Kishkar's chance. He flung the stone at the jackals, grasped his stick firmly and, yelling fiercely, dashed in towards the carcase. With his free hand he grasped the shattered leg with the lump of flesh at the end of it, then, whirling the dead branch threateningly, retreated—fast.

Outraged by this fresh piece of pilfering, the hyena came swiftly round in its crippled, droop-backed manner, hoping to attack from behind. Kishkar wheeled round and caught the animal a clout with the stick that stopped it in its tracks. Then he ran on again, eager to quit the loathsome place. For a while the hyena loped behind him, cringing away whenever Kishkar paused to threaten it; but at last, aware that its rival scavengers were taking advantage of its absence, it went lolloping back to the gruesome feast, and the sound of squabbling continued.

But all Kishkar's efforts were set at nought when, panting and elated, he arrived at the temple. True, Hansia sat up alertly as Kishkar approached with the blackbuck leg so that the boy smiled approvingly—now the cheetah's hunger would be appeased and the danger to Moon Horn be averted.

"I have brought you flesh of your own killing! Feed!" he invited, and placed the carrion in front of Hansia. But to his dismay the cheetah, after having sniffed it curiously, turned away in palpable disdain.

"He has no liking for the jackal's charity," the Jangama observed, poking the carrion towards the cheetah with his staff. Hansia rose and limped to another place, as if feeling contaminated.

Kishkar was downcast at such ingratitude. If the cheetah would not feed, Moon Horn would be in still greater danger. He trembled at the thought of spending another night with the cheetah ravening with hunger, as it surely would be by then. How could he protect Moon Horn?

Now his worries increased.

"There are strangers approaching!" Tipane yelled from where he was guarding Moon Horn.

Kishkar ran to the wall and looked out. Across the sun-battered plain droned the now familiar grinding mutter of a motor-car. In the distance of the dotted bushes and trees rose a pillar of dust.

"It must be the rajah's hunters returning!" he shouted back at Tipane through cupped hand. "Bring Moon Horn into the temple again."

"No!" he corrected himself, with a glance at Hansia. "Drive her down into the thicket over there and wait until I tell you."

At once Tipane did as he was told and drove Moon Horn away out of sight beyond the temple.

Standing by the sun-warmed parapet, where slender lizards scuttled like quicksilver, Kishkar uneasily watched the motor-car come bumping nearer across the corrugated grassland until it reached the smudge of a track that ran towards the temple. There it drove faster, the dust rising in a red veil behind it. Clearly the royal hunters had resumed their search for the cheetah. Perhaps some passing shepherd had given them news. Perhaps somebody had even found tracks leading that way. Kishkar was perturbed. He was afraid the rajah's men would beat him for raiding the picnic, afraid they might hold him responsible for Hansia's injury. He even felt a little sorry, too, that the prince and his servants were coming to fetch away the animal he had befriended.

As he thought this, he saw that Hansia had stood up sharply and was staring through the ruined gateway with its festoon of coral creeper. The cheetah had recognized the sound of the approaching vehicle and awaited its coming expectantly.

Now Kishkar could plainly see the turbanned occupants of the motor-car. He crouched down behind the parapet, for the men were looking up at the temple. The car disappeared round one of the massive walls and Kishkar went scurrying along to the derelict gateway where Hansia stood. He would have liked to stretch out a hand and stroke the cheetah in farewell, but did not dare for fear of being seen. Peeping from behind the stone gate-post, he watched the motor-car draw to a halt. The Prince and two men got out and surveyed the temple, then they began to cast around, searching for tracks. Suddenly one of them exclaimed excitedly and, calling to the prince, pointed.

Down the crumbling steps Hansia went limping. Without a glance at Kishkar, the cheetah made its way towards the men, slowly and with great dignity in spite of its injury.

"Wonder of wonders!" the young prince cried, break-

104

ing into a run. "Here is Hansia in truth. May Allah be praised!"

"She limps, sahib," said one of the attendants. "She is injured."

Hansia the cheetah nuzzled against her master's legs in a frenzy of gladness, while the prince, his brown face alight with pleasure, fondled the animal and murmured caressingly to it. Intently the men examined the cheetah to find its hurt and they stood gathered around, speculating on what had happened.

The prince frowned beneath his blue turban and looked up at the temple. Kishkar was certain he was about to enter the building, but then the young man gave an order and gestured at the car. He was a Moslem and was not interested in a Hindu shrine; besides, the only reason he had come was to trace Hansia, and this he had done. Evidently he was concerned to take the cheetah home as soon as possible so that its wound might be dealt with expertly.

One of the men had fetched a leash and now he snapped it on the cheetah's studded collar. Still talking and gesticulating, they led Hansia to the motor-car, where she imperiously took her accustomed place. The prince climbed into the driving-seat and let in the clutch. Gears crashed, the throbbing engine roared. In a swish of tyres on the sandy ground the vehicle drove off and was rapidly blurred to the watching eye by the curtain of dust.

12 *The Worst Torture of All*

IN the dim avenue of banyan trees, where weird roots dangled from the branches like a hangman's rope, the field-green rhesus monkeys went vaulting and hand-swinging, eager to make the most of their opportunity. Little had passed along the dusty road since the morning, and the monkeys had grown bored to the point of quarrelling among themselves. Now these trudging man-people with the lumbering animal were a welcome target for their abuse and curiosity.

At first the monkeys had merely peeked inquisitively from among the huge leaves or round the massive limbs of the trees, their coppery faces wizened with the frustration monkeys seem to feel because they cannot talk in the human tongue.

The boys and the old man in the yellow robe traipsed on with bowed heads, taking no notice of the monkeys who quizzed them so avidly. For a while even Tipane was too weary to bother about them and clutched his brother's hand as he walked on through the loose, dusty sand of the road.

The monkeys started to show off, busking and leaping skattily across the road, shinning up the banyan ropes and back again in a long agile movement that was like a perpetual grimace. They even forgot their fleas in their anxiety to draw attention to themselves.

When their audience continued to be unappreciative of this talented exhibition, the monkeys started to be abusive. An old male grabbed a handful of little banyan figs and hurled them down. Chattering in admiration at this stroke of genius, the rest of the monkeys followed the example of their elder. A shower of fruit began to rain upon the wayfarers.

Throughout the length of the banyan tunnel the monkeys followed them, keeping up the bombardment. There was no response. The monkeys were holy and must not be harmed. Was there not even a monkey-god of the name of Hanuman? If the monkeys had known that, they would have been unbearable. As it was, the lack of reaction made them more violent than ever. They would dearly have liked the man-people to shout at them, for then they could pretend they were partaking in a dialogue on equal terms with their important relations. But the wayfarers remained maddeningly stoical under the attack and the monkeys became almost hysterical with rage. Some of the young ones lost their balance in their eagerness to score a hit and went screeching and scampering under Moon Horn's hooves.

The Jangama scarcely seemed to notice the antics of the monkeys, except to nod benignly as if at the pranks of so many small children. He had weightier matters to ponder as he limped on, staff in hand. Tipane found it increasingly hard to endure the insults of the monkeys and would have turned to challenge them with stick and stone had not Kishker dragged him on by the hand. But Kishkar frowned, too, as the monkeys vaulted overhead and pelted down the inexhaustible banyan figs, which made Moon Horn shuffle on faster in alarm.

To Kishkar there seemed something cruel in the attacks

of the monkeys. He and Tipane and the Jangama had been obliged to leave the ruined temple in order to seek food and once again they had resumed their weary journey through the dust and the heat. They had marched across the burning scrubland and had come at length to the highway, which led they knew not where. It began to seem to Kishkar that he was condemned for ever to trudge the unfriendly land, and he wondered in despair if there would be any end to his self-imposed exile.

He thought longingly of the Blue Hills as he stumbled on, his eyes fixed on the dusty patterns of the road and the dappling coins of sunlight that fell through the network of branches. What were the People of the Buffalo doing at that moment? Were the young men grappling with the Stone? Were the women filing towards the dairy-temple to collect the milk and the butter-milk? Was Laxam buttering her ringlets, and Sadamut perhaps embroidering a poutkouli? Did they mourn Kishkar and Tipane for dead? Did they even remember Kishkar? For to Kishkar it seemed a matter of years since he fled from the Blue Hills. He could not comprehend that it was still only a matter of days. He did not even feel envious that perhaps Kushken had been appointed Param-joti's acolyte in his place. All he wanted was to return to the friendly, familiar Blue Hills, to run upon the downland turf, crawl on hands and knees through the tiny entrance of his father's hut, enjoy the quiet, slow benison of his home.

But, as if to remind him of why he could not return, Moon Horn turned her muzzle towards Kishkar and gazed at him from her large, velvety eyes. Kishkar nodded in response and placed a hand on the buffalo's shoulder to reassure her. He sighed inwardly, nevertheless. In his

108

mind's eye he saw the Blue Hills and thirsted for their
fragrant coolness and scented blue-gums as a traveller lost
in the desert thirsts for water.

The monkeys seemed to be mocking him. It was as
if they read his thoughts and were jeering that never again
would he return to the homeland he longed for so deeply.

It seemed that the Jangama, too, had read Kishkar's
thoughts, for when at last they emerged from the cool
tunnel of the banyan avenue into the scorching sunlight
and were left in peace the holy man turned and eyed Kishkar as he plodded on, staff in hand.

"The road is long and hot . . . and not even the milk of

a coconut to free the dust from our throats," he said, wiping away some of the cow-dung ash from his forehead, for the sweat had spoilt his Siva marks. "I will tell you a story to entertain you while we march."

"Yes, please tell us," urged Tipane, looking up gladly and moving closer to the Jangama. "What is the story about?"

"We must listen and hear," said Kishkar courteously, while Moon Horn slapped her tail at the pestering flies.

"Once there lived a certain Nizam," the Jangama began, after clearing his throat portentously. "He lived in a beautiful palace inlaid with sandalwood and mother-of-pearl. He owned many wives and many swift horses. . . ."

"He must have been rich indeed," murmured Tipane, tugging at Kishkar's hand, for his brother was not paying attention.

Kishkar smiled as he trudged on alongside Moon Horn. The Jangama thought they were children who must be kept amused.

"But there was one thing more than riches that this great Nizam coveted," the Jangama continued, blinking as a pair of doves flew up from their dust bath in the road. "He desired power over men, not simply the power to order them here and order them there, but power over their souls, too."

"He was very greedy then?" frowned Tipane, not fully understanding.

"Ay, greedy as a vulture," nodded the Jangama. "His appetite was as base as that of the hyena. He had his way in all things. All men grovelled before him, save for one man who withstood him. He refused to acknowledge the greatness of the Nizam. However much the Nizam's servants thrashed him, tortured him, took away his goods, this man steadfastly refused to crawl in the dust at the feet of the rapacious Nizam."

"What was the name of this hero?" asked Tipane with increased interest.

But Kishkar's mind had drifted; he was listening to the persistent *tonk, tonk, tonk* of the coppersmith bird, which seemed to be counting the interminable steps he was fated to take on his trek away from his homeland. . . .

"Murari," the Jangama answered Tipane. "This Murari was indeed a hero, as you say. He defied that abominable Nizam until the Nizam could neither sleep, nor eat anything—except his nails! But then one day a courtier who wished to win favour with his lord compounded a plan. He was as sly as a jackal and cunning as a snake, that courtier was, for he had studied Murari and seen what manner of man he was."

"What did he do?" Tipane demanded, clutching Kishkar's hand more tightly in anticipation of some horror.

"What was his plan?" echoed Kishkar, suddenly interested in the story. He was anxious at the thought that Murari had at last been forced to submit to the Nizam's will.

"It was simple. The Nizam caused Murari to be exiled from home, sent him away from his family and his people. But worse than that, at the suggestion of the courtier he hired a certain sorcerer who was able to send demons to torture the wretched Murari."

"What did the demons do?" Kishkar's voice was thick and husky.

"They whispered in Murari's ear of home", the old man said. "They tormented him with vivid memories of his hearth. The memories were so exquisite, he felt he had only to stretch forth a hand to touch the household things he knew, embrace his wife and children and friends. But, of course, each time his memory burnt to a fever, these visions faded and the unhappy Murari was as parched as a man dying from thirst."

"What happened next?" Tipane asked.

"The Nizam got his way," Kishkar answered for the Jangama. His brown face was blank, his eyes hooded and withdrawn.

"Yes, this was the worst torture of all", agreed the Jangama. "Murari submitted to the Nizam's suzerainty and ever afterwards did his every bidding. As for the courtier, he was amply rewarded for his advice."

"I did not like that man," muttered Tipane. "He was worse than the Nizam for thinking up that plan."

They trudged on in silence, their bare feet ploughing through the dusty furrows of the road. Kishkar fanned Moon Horn's head with a switch of leaves. The Jangama fingered his necklace of rudrashka seeds.

Why had the holy man told this sad story, Kishkar wondered. Wasn't he sad enough already at the thought of home without this salt being rubbed in his wound?

"Ay, in truth," Kishkar said presently, almost to himself, "Murari was indeed an unhappy man. That must be the worst torture of all, to be separated from one's family and people and yet remember it ceaselessly."

"Yes, my son," the Jangama answered eagerly, as if he had been waiting for Kishkar to speak. He halted and leaned on his staff as he faced Kishkar, who halted too. "But you at least are more fortunate than Murari. You are free to return to your hearth at any time. No cruel Nizam detains you. It is you who torture yourself with memories of those Blue Hills of which you have so often spoken—and more often thought."

112

"Yes, let's go home, let's go home," begged Tipane, pulling at Kishkar's arm. But Kishkar ignored him.

"I have told you my story, holy man," Kishkar shook his head. He put a hand protectively on Moon Horn's neck and the heifer stood wearily with lowered head, glad of the chance to rest. "It is because of Moon Horn that I dare not return. I am not afraid for myself." He stood more upright as he spoke. "I will face any punishment the People of the Buffalo shall decree. But I cannot betray Moon Horn, who is of sacred pedigree. She had no part in what happened."

"The buffalo will go to the Shades in the fullness of time," the Jangama pointed out gently. "From what you have told me of the worthy customs of your people, when your father or mother die (may they have long life!), then might this buffalo, the finest in your father's herd because of her sacred pedigree, be sacrificed in order to conduct them into the other world."

"That would be just," agreed Kishkar, though his heart sank. "Moon Horn would acquire great honour through leading my parents into the Shades and I would cast the ceremonial flowers upon her proudly . . . though sadly, too," he added, as he felt Moon Horn's heaving side against his shoulder.

"One night the tiger may take her," the Jangama shrugged, his sunken eyes regarding Kishkar earnestly.

"Still I would not have betrayed Moon Horn," Kishkar answered.

"It is a bad thing to leave one's home," the old man said. "I am old, my body is a husk blown by the wind, a wind which is sent by God. I have taken to the road in search of truth and to give men the benefit of any tiny wisdom God has vouchsafed me, but with you it is different. You are young, your life lies before you. Your place is by your father's side, to bring pride and strength and contentment to your family. Nothing that endures is created without love. Life without the love of one's family and home is like bricks without straw. It crumbles at the first downpour."

Kishkar's eyes were turned to the ground. Why did the holy man torture him? Couldn't he understand that he loved Moon Horn and could not return home while there was danger for her?

"Listen to me, my son," the Jangama persisted, his hands clasped under his chin as they rested on his staff. "This thing happened, ordained by Fate, for there is a pattern in all things, even though its meaning is not at once apparent to us. Only the Great Weaver knows how the pattern is woven. Who knows who sent the snake which started off your misfortune? Was it perhaps the beginning of a pattern designed to test your fortitude or to chasten your pride?"

"But why should Moon Horn, who is innocent, suffer?" Kishkar demanded, sullenly scratching in the dust with his big toe.

"But if you accept that this matter is not simply bad luck," countered the Jangama, "and that it has happened, to the sorrow of all—yourself, your family and your people—then you should earnestly wish to put it right."

"It is too high a price," Kishkar said, leaning against Moon Horn and rubbing a hand along her neck.

"Do not fall into the pit of arrogance, Kishkar," the old man admonished him, though gently. "You are setting your feelings against the well-being of your people. They are affronted because of the theft of their sacred Buffalo Bell. In their eyes only one thing can put this misfortune right. Do you then consider that your feelings and the fate of this buffalo of whom you are so fond weigh in the balance more heavily than the needs of your people?"

Kishkar met the mild eyes of the Jangama that peered at him from beneath his tangled brows. He looked away into the distance of the long road where the heat haze continued its mad, oily dance. In all the days since he had fled from the Blue Hills with Moon Horn and Tipane he had never thought of things as the Jangama showed them to him.

"What is the worst that can happen?" the Jangama asked. "It is that your Moon Horn will fall to the axe. But by her sacrifice she will restore the health of your people who have suffered so great a loss in their eyes. Tell me this, Kishkar, if it were any other buffalo but this one, would you not think it right that, if the Elders of your tribe so decreed, it should be sacrificed to atone for the grievous loss of the Buffalo Bell which is the totem of your people?"

Kishkar sighed and felt Moon Horn's hide flirt as she shook off the flies. He thought that poor Murari in the Jangama's tale had suffered a subtle torture at the hands of those demons of memory that conjured up such alluring visions. But it seemed to him that the need to come to a decision was an even worse torture.

"Come," said the Jangama, trudging on again. He did not press Kishkar for an answer to his question. "We must find food and shelter for the night."

Once again they resumed their apparently endless march along the dusty corridors of the sun. Tipane clutched his brother's hand more tightly and his lip trembled as he hurried to keep up.

13 · *The Bullocks Tread the Grain*

THEY found shelter the following night in a village by the side of a lake, whose shores were fragrant with the scent of frangipani that grew out of the wall of the local temple. The waxen petals like tiny white shallops were beginning to fall upon the water.

Already many other people were there: peasants who had journeyed to the local market to buy or sell oxen and had tarried to drink a cup or two of palm toddy, drivers with diminutive pack donkeys which were laden with vast sacks of millet or cardamons, families which had finished working at the coffee harvest on neighbouring estates, and even some mahouts and their elephants who had been stacking teak logs by the lakeside. There were apothecaries who boiled up the skins of dead snakes as a specific against goitre. There was a man with performing monkeys dressed up in little frocks and adorned with bells. There were beggars with highly profitable sores or mutilated limbs. A barber shaved a man in the open air while spectators watched his artistry. A public letter-writer sat composing an important missive from the stutterings of a bashful peasant. A tailor twirled at a sewing-machine. Everywhere there were people, working or watching others work, pushing and shouting and gesturing.

Kishkar did not like this place. He was afraid for Moon Horn, who was nervous at all the din—the squealing of elephants, the braying of the little donkeys, complaining how their backs ached, the babble of voices as men quarrelled or gambled or gossiped. Even those who slept were not silent, for some of them shrieked in their dreams, while others, their wits muddled by the palm-toddy, uttered nonsense which even the monkeys could have aspired to answer.

Tipane was caught between wonder and terror at the noise and the bustle. The flickering light of roadside fires made every gleaming face look sinister as a demon's; by the market stalls, where ragi, pulse, onions, beads, cloth and sweetmeats were being sold, the reflection of the naphtha flares writhed out like fiery serpents upon the surface of the lake, dimly picking out the huge, sacred mahseer fish that cruised hopefully near the steps of the temple.

While the newcomers hesitated, bemused by the jostling throng, an old peasant of the sect of Siva caught sight of the Jangama.

"Make way, make way there!" he shouted, pushing a path through the white-clad loiterers. "Make way for an honoured guest who has come to grace my threshold!"

Smiling and nodding, he made namasta repeatedly to the Jangama, walking backwards before him, careless of whose toes he trod on or whose ribs his elbows bruised in his eagerness to gain favour with the holy man, who tottered wearily after him.

"Keep back, worthless beggars that I see you are!" the man ordered Kishkar, waving a hand at him. "You are not worthy to keep company with this holy man!"

"This boy and his brother have shared the bread of companionship with me," said the Jangama, firmly. "He, too, is a seeker after the truth as I am. His buffalo heifer is of a sacred line, even as Nandi, the riding-bull of Siva. You must give shelter to all who are with me or none."

"My ox-stall is empty, holy man!" the peasant cried, changing his tune at once. "I have lent my bullocks to my uncle. The boy's animal shall rest in the stall and I will bring it a bundle of paddy-straw to eat. . . ."

"But not a very big one," he thought.

So Kishkar saw Moon Horn installed in the little thatched shelter at the side of the dwelling, after which the man led the guests into his home, having first driven away sundry goats and pariah dogs and pot-bellied black pigs that crowded about the doorway.

"Woman!" he ordered grandly, clapping his hands at his wife. "Bring food. See, the holy man of Siva has journeyed from afar solely to visit the home of Khoroo. We shall acquire great virtue through our hospitality. . . ."

118

He glanced dubiously at the two brothers. The brats looked greedy as vultures. He hoped his hospitality would not cost him too much.

Kishkar did not take to the man Khoroo with his unctuous manner, or to the way he fawned on the Jangama. Still, the kheer of rice and milk that the woman brought was good and nourishing and the curried tree-tomatoes were succulent. Tipane was so weary that he fell asleep almost as soon as he had finished his supper. Kishkar carried him to a corner of the hut and wrapped him in the embroidered robe. He, too, was glad to stretch out on the earth floor, while Khoroo plagued the old man with senseless chatter and various neighbours squatted at the threshold to see the illustrious visitor.

Kishkar did not sleep. His mind was too full of what the Jangama had said to him on the road that day. He lay awake gazing up at the bamboo thatch where the chik-chak lizards scuttled and called. His thoughts churned round and round inside his head, like a team of bullocks treading out the corn. And like the bullocks, Kishkar's thoughts, too, were as if blindfold; however much he considered the matter he could not arrive at a decision.

Long after the neighbours had taken their leave and the Jangama had lain down to rest, Kishkar remained awake thinking and listening to the gentle breathing of Moon Horn in the ox-stall outside and the occasional rustle of straw.

Gradually the village grew silent. The toddy-drinkers fell into a dull slumber. The gamblers put away their greasy cards and forgot their quarrels over their game of gunn. Even the elephants ceased to blast the night with their longings for the jungle. The distant plaint of jackals, the furtive scavenging of dogs, the gnawing of a porcupine, the ripple of water at the lakeside, the occasional cry of some sleeper: such puny sounds were merely scratchings on the bell-jar of silence that descended over the sleeping village.

Kishkar longed for home. He edged nearer to Tipane and pressed his face into the folds of his robe, which was tattered and stained now through much journeying. He almost cried out as if with pain as the demons of memory tortured him as they had tortured Murari in the Jangama's tale.

Was the Jangama right in his reasoning, or would it be a cowardly betrayal of Moon Horn to seize the excuse the old man's counsel offered? Restlessly his weary brain moved round like those blindfold oxen as he strove to reach a decision. It would have been so easy to be tempted. To feel again the caressing downland turf beneath his feet, to breathe the fragrance of gorse flowers and blue-gums instead of the sun-jaded air of these crowded lands where every man suspected his neighbour. To drink again the life-giving milk, joke with Sadamut as she came past from the dairy-temple, listen to the words of his father. All this could be restored to him . . . at a price. He knew he must be convinced before he paid that price.

At last, exhausted by his thoughts, Kishkar fell asleep, while outside the fireflies flitted across the spicy darkness.

He did not wake until the chill of the dawn stole across the lake in a grey vapour and made a filigree of the frangipani branches. Through the unglazed window of the house he could see the shape of a woman moving like a wraith to fetch water.

Vaguely Kishkar could hear voices somewhere close by and, leaning on an elbow, he saw the Jangama squatting with bowed head in the doorway, silhouetted against the pervading greyness. Out of sight a man talked earnestly

120

to him and Khoroo was apparent by his noisy throat-clearing.

"My child will die, holy man, if you do not come," the stranger was murmuring deferentially.

"Your fame has spread far since you graced my humble hearth," put in Khoroo. "This man Makhana is my cousin. He has come from the other side of the lake. There were men here yesterday for the cattle market. They took back news of your coming. . . . Keep thy distance, though, Makhana."

"Since when has the child been affected by the Maharani?" asked the Jangama, pulling his robe over his bare shoulder. He meant that the child had small-pox, which, as everyone knew, was caused by the anger of the goddess, Seetla Maharani.

"Three days now, holy man," Makhana replied, in a low voice, "I have done all that is ordained. I have not shaved. My wife has offered water morning and evening to the goddess."

"It is a bold thing to dare the anger of the Maharani," said the Jangama, fingering his rudrashka beads. "Have you made sure not to cook vegetables in kettles or saucepans and not to use oil or ghee for cooking?"

"Yes, yes, all this I have seen to," Makhana said urgently. "I will reward you fittingly if you save my daughter."

"Do not forget me either, Makhana," said Khoroo in an undertone, but sharply. "The holy man was dwelling in my home when you came for him. You will make a little gift?"

"I will not forget," Makhana assured him. "I have some kalami mangoes ripening under a stack of paddy-straw. You shall have some."

The Jangama levered himself up with his staff and the men began to make their way towards the lake, where the snake birds and the egrets were tilting impatiently to and fro as if hoping to disperse the grey pall that hindered their fishing.

For a moment Kishkar paused, for the bullocks had begun to trample round in his brain once more. Then, careful not to disturb Tipane, who still slept, he went pattering out of the house, past the sleepers huddled under their carts by the ashes of last night's noisy fires.

At the lakeside the Jangama was about to step into the frail little raft-boat of bamboo that Makhana had sculled across in. Kishkar flung himself down and placed first one, then the other of the old man's feet on his forehead, as if the Jangama were his father. The Jangama looked down keenly at Kishkar and his eyes searched the boy's, as if to see what kind of grain those bullocks had trampled out.

"You do not come with me, Kishkar," he stated rather than asked. "It seems that this boat was not built to carry such as Moon Horn and her friends," he added, with a little smile that twitched among the etched wrinkles of his face.

Suddenly, kneeling there by the water's edge, where the fat mahseer swirled hungrily, Kishkar felt that fate had provided him with the solution to the problem that tormented him. It seemed to him that there was something meaningful in the Jangama's departing like this across the lake. He could not accompany the old man: he must turn back. He had made his decision kneeling there in the cold grey dawn which the liquid gold of sunrise was beginning to disperse.

"No, holy man," he answered gravely, getting to his

feet. "I do not come with you. I have journeyed far enough. Now I must return to my father's house."

"You speak wisely, Kishkar," the old man nodded, as, with Khoroo's helping hand, he squatted in the tiny boat, where the water lapped through the bamboo-poles. "God's blessing be on you and your people. May the pattern be woven well."

Now Makhana began to scull quickly away from the shore, while the snake birds and the egrets screamed joyfully, their wings touched with gold as the sun came surging up above the distant jungle.

For a while Kishkar stood with Khoroo, watching the boat grow smaller. He felt sad at parting from the Jangama; their companionship at that moment had been far deeper than during all the time they had been together. But he felt grateful to the old man for having made him see what was right. He knew now that he had come to the right decision, despite the peril that confronted Moon Horn. It was his duty to return to the Blue Hills for the good of the People.

As Kishkar stood there, Tipane came stumbling from the house, knuckling the sleep from his eyes. He ran down to the shore and put a hand in his brother's.

14 *The Pattern is Woven*

When Makhana's little craft was small as a dabchick on the steel mirror of the lake, Kishkar and Tipane went to fetch Moon Horn from the ox-stall. She thrust out her head as usual for Kishkar to rub it, and her great tongue rasped affectionately along his arm.

"Enough!" Kishkar said, with unwonted harshness and pushed the buffalo's head away. "We have far to go. . . ."

"We are going home!" Tipane cried, leaning against Moon Horn and looking at his brother with difficulty above the heifer's neck. "Aren't you glad? We shall run fast as a hunting-leopard all the way. We are going home! I'm not tired any more."

Kishkar said nothing, but led Moon Horn out of the stall. By the time they returned to the lake to let her drink at the water's edge, where the dhobi-men were beginning their laundry, the bamboo boat had vanished altogether, taking the Jangama on his errand to stay the Seetla Maharani's anger.

Kishkar was sure the Jangama's faith and skill would cure the little girl. It was strange to think that if by chance, too weary to press on, they had stayed the night in some other place, the Jangama would not have been there to go to the aid of Makhana's daughter. But it was part of his pattern that he should have come to Khoroo's house that night.

When they had washed Moon Horn thoroughly, grooming her hide with fallen burrs until it shone sleekly, Kishkar and Tipane led the dripping heifer past the walls of the local temple, whose time-blunted carvings of fish were as vague as the mahseer in the lake itself. Kishkar noticed a bush of jasmine near the steps and, leaving Moon Horn and his brother for a moment, picked a few sprigs of the delicately scented flowers. The temple was not of his faith, the Hindus had other gods than great Ouen, but Makhana's little girl was a Hindu, so perhaps it would be a good thing if he took the flowers to the temple as an offering for her recovery.

But when he approached the gateway a shaven-headed priest suddenly appeared, with three striped caste marks on his forehead and wearing the Brahmin's sacred thread from his left shoulder to his right hip. His face contorted with horror as he caught sight of Kishkar mounting the steps, on which the gathering sun threw the boy's shadow. He held out an agitated hand and backed away as if afraid, shouting scoldingly as he did so.

At this another man darted out from the temple, yelling even more fiercely. At first Kishkar stood bewildered with the flowers in his hand, but then he understood. The priest had taken his ritual bath and would be polluted even by so much as Kishkar's shadow. It was not for the likes of Kishkar to set foot inside that holy place.

He made namasta apologetically to the angry priests and, leaving the little spray of jasmine on the steps, ran back to Moon Horn and Tipane, abashed now at his own presumption. All the same, he still hoped the Jangama was in time to save the life of Makhana's daughter.

"Shall I throw a stone at them?" whispered Tipane, angry for his brother's sake. Tipane seemed to have changed from a child to a boy since Kishkar told him they were going home. It was as if, turning about, he had scented the air of the distant Blue Hills and had been strengthened. "I don't like such priests. They are not happy like the Jangama."

"Even though they are cleaner," he added, as an after-thought.

"Come, it is still far to go," said Kishkar, catching his brother by the arm before he should disgrace them, ". . . even at the pace of the hunting-leopard."

He was glad to quit the strident, jangling village, where the people were stirring, lighting their cow-dung fires, preparing their cooking-pots, yoking their bullocks to the creaking carts, haggling over a few coffee beans or a measure of rice.

Did it make sense, *his* pattern, he wondered, as he and Tipane led Moon Horn along the road, where the pack-donkeys and their drovers slouched. He was turning his steps homeward, to the Blue Hills, to submit to the judge-ment of his people. This he could have done without all the weary journeying, the discomfort and anxiety that he and Tipane had gone through. When Laxam ran across the downs that far-off evening to tell him of the findings of the Council of Elders, he could have bowed to their decision without more ado instead of fleeing, only to return after all these days. He knew now that he was not betraying Moon Horn. He knew that, though he might be leading the buffalo back to her death, he was doing right. The welfare of his people was more important than any-thing else. The loss of the Buffalo Bell must be atoned for —or worse evil might befall.

The Jangama had said there was a pattern in all things, even if you could not understand it to begin with. But

126

Kishkar could not help feeling that what he had done was as futile as a pattern that is unravelled by pulling on a loose thread. . . .

Hardly aware of Tipane's chatter, he walked sombre-eyed along the road, between the terraced paddy-fields where the cumbersome water-buffaloes staggered at the plough, under the same fierce sun that had battered him day after day, and breathing the same acrid dust. But he knew he was right to turn back. He would brace his shoulders against the sneers and mockery of Kushken; he would allow no tears to fall from his eyes when the sledge-hammer crashed down on Moon Horn's brow. But he would wait for the day, however distant, when he would rejoin Moon Horn in the cool land of the Shades.

From time to time Kishkar glanced questioningly at Moon Horn. Did she sense what had happened? That they were returning to her certain death? Moon Horn's fine head seemed to sink lower under the splendid horns, as if it felt already the weight of Kunparadi's death-blow. Her ribs stood out like the shell of a boat, for even in those few days Moon Horn had tasted the starvation diet of the plains, where men's religion prevented them from slaying their cattle but allowed them to condemn the animals to a living death for lack of pasture.

When they had been walking for much of the sultry morning, they came upon a little group of people trailing slowly along, seeking the shade of the trees. They moved so wearily that despite the ambling pace of Moon Horn the brothers soon caught up with them: a woman in a green sari, a boy of about the same age as Tipane, and an old man, the grandfather no doubt, carrying a small child on his shoulders.

They eyed the brothers curiously, as all people did, for

127

it was clear that Kishkar and Tipane were not of those parts. But they were friendly enough, for the bond of weariness is always strong, and Kishkar was glad of their company.

"That is a fine beast you have," the old man remarked, padding on bandy-legged under the weight of the child, who stared down listlessly. "Have you brought her from the market at Harimalli? I saw no such cattle yesterday."

"Such cattle as ours are not sent to market," Tipane answered boldly, glancing at the other boy as if daring him to challenge this proud statement.

"By my eye!" the woman exclaimed, when she had discovered where Kishkar had come from. "You have journeyed far from your home. Does not your mother weep bitter tears for you?"

Kishkar frowned and shrugged. More than ever he knew he was right to turn back.

"And you who walk with the stride of the giant Ravana, who carried off Seeta, the wife of Ram," the woman smiled at Tipane. "You are no older than my Shudraka here, yet you are so far from home."

"We are getting nearer with every step we take," Tipane replied stoutly.

The old grandfather walked more slowly than ever and presently came to a halt, his legs quaking visibly.

"It is as well that we have not such a journey in front of us," he declared, lifting the child down from his bowed shoulders and setting it on the ground. "I can carry Lakshmi no farther."

"The child is sick," the woman muttered, lowering the sack she was carrying. "She cannot walk by herself."

"You have far to go?" asked Kishkar, pausing with a hand on Moon Horn's neck.

128

"To where the two roads join," the woman told him. "My man is chief sawyer at the saw-pits. I and my father travelled to the market to buy salt and rice."

"Give me the child," Kishkar offered, holding out his hands. Stooping, he caught hold of Lakshmi and swung her on to his shoulders. He had felt weary himself, but somehow it refreshed him to be able to help these people who were even wearier than he. With the child astride his shoulders he paused now and again to wait for them as they plodded on, while Tipane helped Shudraka carry his sack of rice.

The sawyer's camp was a mile or two along the road and before long the laboured shriek of a saw could be heard above the din of cicadas and the ridiculous refrain of the brain-fever bird. The sawyers were cutting into planks a massive tree trunk that was straddled across a scaffolding of posts erected in the saw-pit. While the top sawyer worked overhead on the scaffolding, his assistant laboured in the pit and his glossy, almost black skin was coated with sawdust and sweat.

The sawyers willingly stopped work when their family returned and soon a pot of rice was steaming above a fire of shavings. Shudraka beckoned Tipane and led him to a grove of coconut trees above the road. Nimbly he began to climb one of them, appearing almost to run up the graceful bole, and threw down several of the hairy, heavy fruit. When he descended he took a cutty-knife from the sawyer, his father, and deftly sliced off the tops.

"Drink!" he invited, with a smile red from betel-nut, and gave the brothers each a coconut.

"Sit and we will eat," said the woman to Kishkar, as she tended the cooking-pot. "You are welcome to such as we have in gratitude. You have carried my ingot of gold for me," she smiled, turning a glance at Lakshmi, whom she had laid on some gunny-sacks in the shade. But first Kishkar was anxious to let Moon Horn drink, for the air was tense and oppressive, and thunder muttered beyond the horizon. So Shudraka showed him a little rivulet near which was some grass that would give the heifer a mouthful of food.

From the sawyer's camp they could look down on the junction of the two roads, and while they squatted there eating they watched the passers-by and the traffic—herds of bleating, long-eared sheep, bullock-carts, an occasional motor-car that churned the red dust into smoke, and once a company of English soldiers on horseback, who waved cheerily to them and shouted out.

Presently, along the road from the direction of the village where Kishkar and Tipane had spent the night came another motor-car, followed by a ramshackle country bus. At the same time a team of pink-faced, dust-plastered working-elephants appeared on the side road, ambling towards the fork. From the opposite direction came a two-wheeled tonga-cart drawn briskly by a little horse with flowing mane.

All this traffic converged on the fork of the roads at the same time and nobody seemed to realize that it was necessary for someone to give way. The leading mahout was asleep anyway and his elephant continued to amble ponderously on, unconcerned with lesser beings. The tonga swerved to pass round the elephant, while the approaching motor-car in turn pulled over violently to avoid a head-on collision with the horse. It pulled over too abruptly, and before the driver could recover the motor-car had lurched with a shattering crash of metal against rock into the monsoon ditch at the side of the road.

130

Uproar ensued. The elephants squealed in alarm, the mahouts awoke and started to shout, the horse neighed and the driver of the tonga brandished his whip in agitation. The bus braked abruptly to a standstill and the driver yelled shrill comments from the window. Out of the damaged motor-car a white man clambered and he shouted loudest of all, shaking a fist at the world in general.

"Aiee!" Kishkar could not suppress the gasping cry of astonishment that burst from him. He sprang up from the fire and moved a pace or two nearer the road. His heart was beating uncomfortably and he stared for a long time to make certain that what his eyes told him was true. For the white sahib who stood angrily arguing with the driver of the tonga was the same fat tourist who had violated the dairy-temple and stolen the sacred Buffalo Bell.

15 *The Thread is Broken*

IT was a fine spectacle. What was more, it cost nothing. You didn't see a motor-car every day, and you certainly didn't see one crash into a ditch very often.

Although the accident had happened in the middle of the countryside, it was astonishing how quickly a delighted crowd collected. There were the mahouts and the tonga-driver to begin with, then the sawyer's family left their camp-fire and the passengers clambered down from the bus to get a better look at the extraordinary sight of that shining, important motor-car lying on its side in the monsoon gully. People seemed to pop up from nowhere, for the road all at once was crowded with passers-by and cattle and ox-carts. Nobody was in a hurry, nobody minded if he was held up all day. There was all the time in the world to sit and smoke or chew betel-nut and chatter about the mishap. Everybody enjoyed the spectacle, except the

132

white sahib and his mem-sahib and the tonga-driver, who was deeply apprehensive.

And Kishkar. Enjoyment did not come into the matter as far as he was concerned. With a painful tightness at his chest, he stood by the roadside in bewildered amazement and watched the white tourist. All the incidents of the past, weary, distressing days flooded back through his mind. He saw again his father talking by the fireside of Paramajoti choosing Kishkar to guard the dairy-temple. He saw the contest with the temple stone, the stately dance of the Elders. He heard again that piercing scream as Sadamut was confronted by the cobra.

He trembled, his eyes swam, he was oblivious to the babble around him. All he could think was that this fat white man in the drill suit and the topee, standing only a few paces from him, was the cause of all his misery and of all the indignity that had befallen the People of the Buffalo.

But what was Kishkar to do? Accuse the white sahib? Tell someone what had happened and ask their help? Where was the Buffalo Bell? Did the tourist still have it— in the motor-car—in his luggage?

Meanwhile, the tourist continued to gesticulate and talk angrily, while his mem-sahib, having dusted herself down and powdered her face, stared disdainfully at the ring of dark faces as if they did not exist. For a moment the tourist turned and looked straight at Kishkar, who instinctively pressed back a little among the people around him. But it was plain that the tourist did not recognize him; he was too busy complaining bitterly of his predicament. He took off his topee, wiped his brow with a silk handkerchief, and continued his verbal abuse of the tonga-driver. An elephant raised its trunk and trumpeted significantly.

Kishkar could understand only a few words of what the

white sahib was saying, but one of the bus passengers had taken it upon himself to provide a running commentary for the benefit of the assembled audience.

"This sahib is a most important gentleman," he said loudly, gesturing with his umbrella and talking in a sing-song voice. "He will make this ass of a tonga-driver pay dearly for his error. . . ."

"It was the mahout who was at fault!" shrilled the tonga-driver, raising a threatening hand at the elephants. "He should have waited until the road was clear."

"My Rajendra gives way to nobody," the mahout answered back from on high, while the pink-faced elephant surreptitiously examined the contents of the tonga with his trunk. "He would eliminate your spavined horse with one touch of his foot!"

Many people joined in the argument in half a dozen tongues, from Hindi to English, while the white sahib continued to complain in his bull-like voice.

"The sahib is much pressed for time," the man with the umbrella continued, as if he were delivering a speech. "He was driving to the rajah's airfield at Animalli when this upset to his plans occurred!"

"Harness the elephants to the motor-car and haul it out!" suggested somebody. The driver of an ox-team came forward to offer his services (at a good price) to the white sahib. But it was obvious that even if the motor-car could be dragged back on to the road it was probably too badly damaged for the tourists to continue their journey in it.

A long and agitated discussion began between the sahib and his wife and their servant. They were clearly worried about the time and they turned presently to speak to the bus-driver.

134

"The sahib has decided to travel by the bus," announced the man with the umbrella. "They are most important people. They will travel by the rajah's aeroplane. Aeroplane, that is machine with wings that flies at great height," he added thoughtfully for the more ignorant onlookers.

"The rajah is very modern-minded," put in someone else. "He has motor-cars also."

Now the bus-driver and the white man's servant began to transfer the luggage from the motor-car. Two or three suitcases and valises were lifted out.

"Very rich man, this sahib, you see. Honourable Horace Tomkins, he is called," the umbrella man whispered dramatically, as he squinted at one of the labels.

Kishkar watched in growing tension. The Buffalo Bell was assuredly packed in one of those shining suitcases now being loaded on the bus. Grunting, the servant and the bus-driver humped them on their backs and struggled up the little iron ladder at the rear of the bus. In a few moments the white tourist would vanish, and Kishkar would never see him again. It would signify nothing, the fact that he had encountered him on the road like this.

What could he do? He must, he must do something! Urgently he pushed among the crowd, looking for Tipane. He heard the passengers chattering shrilly as they clambered up again to take their seats. He heard the clattering rumble of the engine starting.

"Tipane!" he shouted, as he caught sight of Tipane and Shudraka standing on a rock to get a better view of the spectacle.

"Climb up here with us!" screeched Tipane, jumping about excitedly. "There is a fine view here! You can see everything! The white sahib has got into the bus! He has bribed the driver to drive very fast!"

"Yes, we heard him, it is true!" Shudraka corroborated, jumping about, too, until he and Tipane had to clutch each other fearfully to stop themselves tumbling from the rock.

"Tipane!" shouted Kishkar, above the din. "Listen to me! It is very important! I have got to go. You must stay with Shudraka and his family and look after Moon Horn until I return."

"But why? I am coming with you!" cried Tipane, starting to lower himself from the rock.

"You must do as I say!" ordered Kishkar. "I can't explain now!"

He hurried back through the crowd, for the bus was moving off. It passed him in a stink of petrol and an explosion of dust. The people stepped hurriedly out of its way and Kishkar could not force his way through in time. He dodged round the crowd, darted between the tonga-cart and the elephants. The bus was gathering speed. Kishkar ran as fast as he could, choked and blinded by fumes and dust. He did not know what he was going to do. He was afraid of that bus roaring uncouthly ahead of him, and was prepared to believe it was a living monster capable of rounding on him in its wrath. But he had to catch up with it. Nothing else mattered. Despairingly he stretched out a hand, grabbed hold of a rung of the iron ladder. His arm was almost wrenched from its socket. Then he grabbed with his other hand and jumped, blindly, recklessly, unable to see properly in the swirling dust, but he found a foothold on the lowest rung of the little ladder and crouched there fearfully, eyes shut, lungs heaving.

With toe and hand he clung on precariously. His arms ached abominably, and the iron ladder bruised the soles of his feet. Every time the bus crashed over a pothole his body was jarred with pain. Once he opened his eyes but

136

shut them again hurriedly, for the dusty road seemed to surge up to meet him.

The bus went increasingly faster—the bus-driver had been well paid by the white sahib. Sometimes, going round a bend in the road the driver had to brake violently and Kishkar was flung against the iron ladder.

This was the first time in his life that Kishkar had ever travelled by motor vehicle, and he did not want to do so again. Battered, bruised, jolted, breathless, unable even to think, he clamped his arms up round the iron rung, locked his hands together and crouched there, red with dust from head to foot.

How long that journey lasted, how far it was, where it led, Kishkar had no idea at all. With clenched teeth and tense muscles, he simply clung on: that was all he could think about. It was no longer a question of staying on the bus because of the tourist—he knew that if he let go now he would probably be killed.

He shuddered every time he opened his eyes and looked down at the ugly road streaming beneath him through the red veil. At times it seemed as if he were in some hideous nightmare, being dragged along by an insatiable juggernaut to his doom.

And then suddenly it was all over. Lurching and crashing, the bus swerved off the road, through a wire gateway. The dust ceased to swirl, the wheels ceased to thunder over the potholes and gullies, and the bus went rolling smoothly along a wide strip of concrete. It was like emerging into calm water after a storm.

The bus came to a standstill outside a long wooden building from which one or two men in uniform strolled. Kishkar hopped off quickly and limped away before anyone could question him. He felt giddy from the fumes, but he had to keep watch and follow the tourist. Farther away he saw a little aeroplane. He had never before seen an aeroplane, but he guessed that was what it was. Those two-winged machines that flew like birds were some sort of white man's magic.

All the passengers followed the Honourable Tomkins Sahib and his mem-sahib out of the bus. They would all be late, for the bus-driver had made a detour of several miles for the convenience of the tourists, but the passengers did not mind. It was an adventure, for few of them had seen an aeroplane close to and it made them feel important to be in the same bus that had brought the white man specially to fly in the rajah's private aeroplane.

"That machine flies at one hundred and fifty miles an hour," declared the man with the umbrella, who led the procession in the wake of the Honourable Horace. "Most excellent machine, that. A Rapide, they call it."

"I would not like to fly in it," muttered another man. "I am of the opinion that it would anger the gods to fly heavenwards so high."

"Yes," agreed someone else. "The storm is coming, too. One would be well advised to make powerful puja before one dared such a thing."

It was true: the storm that had been threatening all day was now piling up in vast cumulus clouds beyond the horizon of the little airfield. Thunder rumbled like an ox-cart, and a purple streak of lightning flickered above the palm trees beyond the runway.

Meanwhile, another white man had greeted the tourists, who with gestures and loud laughter explained what had happened.

"If you could have seen that tonga-driver's face. He really thought he was in for a lambasting. . . ."

138

"I hired the car from a chap in Mysore. Could you get the thing seen to, like a good chap. . . ."

"We are so frightfully grateful to His Highness for putting his plane at our disposal. . . ."

"I'm afraid the weather report is pretty ropey. Think we ought to wait till later?"

"No, no. Must press on and all that. . . ."

Everything was all right now. The Honourable Tomkins was very different from what he had been when the accident happened. He laughed continuously and slapped his thigh and patted the officer on the shoulder. The mem-sahib, too, smiled graciously and showed her big white teeth.

"You see," explained the knowledgeable man with the umbrella. "English women wear gold in their teeth, unlike our womenfolk, who wear it in their noses. But it is valuable, all the same."

With great daring, Kishkar went over to the bus again. The white man's bearer had climbed up the iron ladder and was lowering the luggage to two sweepers who had come from the airfield building. Tomkins shouted an order to the bearer, who in turn shouted at the sweepers.

Once again Kishkar found himself surveying the handsome suitcases. Once again he trembled inwardly at the thought that one of them contained the Buffalo Bell. He glanced round in despair. There was nobody to whom he could turn. Should he go to the officer—he looked a kindly man in spite of his fierce moustaches—and tell him? He didn't dare! They would laugh at him or, worse, beat him. How could he accuse a white sahib?

But he must act! In a few moments it would be too late. Already the sweepers were staggering towards the aeroplane, the suitcases loaded on their heads. Now another white man in uniform had appeared, carrying a kind of helmet with goggles. He saluted affably and shook hands with the Honourable and Mrs Tomkins and more talk went on. The officer surveyed the lowering sky and shrugged. They all began to walk towards the aeroplane.

"That is the pilot," explained the man with the umbrella. "He steers the aeroplane—with a joystick. Like this," and he gave a demonstration with his umbrella. "I know all this. My wife's cousin is mechanic."

"The storm is getting worse," said the bus-driver, wincing as another streak of lightning hissed across the sky. A dry hot wind rose up from the airfield.

All the passengers followed the group of white people towards the aeroplane. Kishkar hurried at the edge of the crowd, stifled with uncertainty. In the side of the aeroplane a door had been opened, and the sweepers were climbing up a step ladder to hand the luggage into the aircraft.

How could he stop it? What could he do? Cling on to the tail of the aeroplane as he had clung on to the bus?

"Get back out of the way, all you people!" the first officer shouted in Hindi. "You shouldn't be here anyway. Stand well clear!"

"We must watch from here," said the man with the umbrella. "The aeroplane is about to take off. Stand by for action!"

In dull resignation Kishkar watched. The pilot and the tourists had vanished inside the aircraft. With a mighty roar the engine broke into life. The propeller whirred like a huge insect gone mad. The bus passengers stared in wonder, trod on each other's toes, clapped hands to their ears.

Slowly the little aeroplane taxied down the runway.

140

Quickly it gathered speed. It hesitated, staggered, then rose in the air. Its wings tilted, it rose steadily higher, it circled the airfield and came back roaring loudly overhead. The bus passengers cowered in alarm, all except the man with the umbrella who stood firm with a superior smile on his lips, though he blinked his eyes somewhat.

Soon the aeroplane was no more than a speck as it turned north towards the towering clouds. Kishkar felt empty as a dry gourd as he watched it go. It would have been better had he never encountered the tourist again. Surely the gods were mocking him.

Overhead the thunder crashed more brutally than ever. A swift sword of lightning cleft the oppressive air. Huge raindrops began to patter down.

16 *Storm over the Blue Hills*

KISHKAR squatted under the wall of the airfield building. He was indifferent to everything around him. The purple whip-cracks of lightning, the tumbling load of logs that seemed continually to be falling from an ox-cart in the sky, the grey perpendicular rain that descended in a sheet of enormous drops, so numerous that their individual sound merged into a steady roar: none of this did Kishkar see or hear.

He did not even have his embroidered cloak to comfort him, for he had left it behind at the sawyer's camp. Not even when the Buffalo Bell was stolen and he had been disgraced, had he felt so wretched, so hopeless. That had been grievous enough, unjust as it was, but this last mockery was far worse. His hopes had been raised and then dashed—as if he had been lifted bodily on giant wings to survey some divine view, only to be thrown down in contempt. The gods were indeed mocking him, to bring him and the tourist face to face, only to allow the thief to fly off unscathed. Kishkar's grief was bitter. Had he not been punished enough already, without this final savage cut?

"Where is the Jangama's pattern now?" he thought, a listless, far-off expression in his eyes. It seemed like a pattern pulled and tangled by a wanton child.

On to the veranda of the building came the white

officer with the big moustaches. He leaned on the railing and pursed his lips dubiously as he looked at the chaotic sky. Then he glanced down and noticed Kishkar.

"What are you doing down there?" he demanded, in bad Hindi. "You can wait on the veranda till the storm blows over."

Kishkar made namasta. He didn't much care whether he sheltered from the rain or not. But he did not like to appear ungrateful, so he got up and sat a little to one side of the veranda steps, his body streaming with raindrops.

Now a peon in white shirt and shorts emerged from another door and stood near the white officer. "Bad weather, sahib," he said, as the thunder unrolled high overhead. "Bad for flying."

"Too true," agreed the officer, bracing his back as he leaned with his hands on the rail, watching the fusillade of rain. "Won't be surprised if they have to turn back. Shouldn't have gone. But Tomkins Sahib would have it. Weather report's bad. Especially over the Blue Hills area. . . ."

He chewed his moustache, looked at his watch and hummed tunelessly. He turned sharply as somebody called him from the office doorway. Another Hindu in drill uniform hurried towards him, holding out a sheet from a signal pad.

"Sahib!" the man cried. "Radio message from Captain Holden. Forced to turn back, sahib. Weather impossible. Bad electric storm over the Blue Hills. He says too difficult."

"Well, I'm not surprised," said the officer, scanning the message. "They ought never to have set off. Tomkins Sahib won't be best pleased. But he'll have to lump it."

None of this did Kishkar understand, for it was in English.

143

What he did understand presently was that the airfield men were preparing for an aeroplane to arrive, yet even then he squatted where he was, indifferent to what was going on.

Frail as a leaf the little aircraft skimmed down out of the hostile sky. But only when he saw who had arrived in the returning aeroplane did fire come into Kishkar's eyes again, and the blood that had been cold in his veins run hot and eager once more. For he saw that the passengers whom the airfield staff had gone to meet with huge umbrellas were the same tourist and his wife.

What strange hand was at work on the pattern all this time? The thread had not been broken after all!

He sprang to his feet and moved unobtrusively out of the way as the party arrived at the veranda. Tomkins Sahib was talking loudly, his ruddy complexion a shade paler than usual. Evidently he had not enjoyed his brief flight. His mem-sahib was glad to lean on the white officer's arm.

"You were perfectly right, Baring," Tomkins Sahib said, rather graciously, as if he were conferring a favour. "We shouldn't have taken off. Of course, if I'd realized the weather was going to get worse. . . ."

"I did point out, sir," Baring murmured.

"Yes, yes, I know. But I thought we would run out of it, you know. Anyway, here we are again, thanks to Holden."

"What d'you propose to do now, sir?" asked Baring, as they all stood on the veranda and the bearers folded the enormous umbrellas.

"Think the weather will clear before nightfall?" Tomkins Sahib asked.

"I refuse to fly again until the weather is perfectly safe," his mem-sahib declared in a languid but determined voice. "You will have to get in touch with His Highness, Horace. He will be only too glad to put us up at the palace again, I'm sure."

"Maybe that will be the best thing," muttered the Honourable Tomkins, glancing idly at the huddled figure at the end of the veranda. "Look here, Baring. Can you telephone the palace and explain what has happened? Speak to Ameer Nath, the major-domo, or whatever he calls himself, and put him in the picture."

"I will do that, sir," agreed Baring Sahib, a little stiffly. He didn't see why he should make excuses for Tomkins, who had been so obstinate. If anything had happened to the aircraft, Baring would have had to answer for it to the rajah. "I'll lay on a car to take you to the palace as soon as I've got through to them. But while we're waiting, please come into my office. I am sure Mrs Tomkins would like to rest for a bit."

"I would simply adore a cup of tea," said the mem-sahib.

Wet and cold, but alert, Kishkar had no clear notion of the matters that were being discussed, but he watched keenly when the luggage was brought into the building. Presently, when a motor-car came splashing round to the veranda steps, he listened to the airfield staff and the Honourable Tomkins's bearer talking together as they loaded the suitcases into the boot.

"By my youth!" the bearer said impressively. "I did not think to set foot on earth again."

"I would not travel in a flying-machine if it were a Garuda bird bearing the Lord Vishnu," said one of the sweepers, chewing his betel-nut quid in agitation at the thought.

"It was nothing," boasted the bearer, shoving another case in. "My master joked constantly during the storm. But the mem-sahib, she smelt all the time at a little bottle that gives reviving strength."

They chattered on and at length all the luggage was stowed. In due course Tomkins Sahib and his wife, together with Baring and Holden, emerged. Once again there were handshakes and salutes and pleasant conversation.

"Thank you so much! We've been a frightful bore!"

"Not in the least. A pleasure."

"See you at the palace this evening, no doubt?"

The car doors slammed, the engine thrummed smoothly, and the bearer hopped in next to the driver.

"To the Mohana Palace!" he ordered and sat there importantly with folded arms, while the driver let in the clutch and the motor-car glided off with a hissing of water that spurted out from under the tyres.

Once again Kishkar watched Tomkins Sahib and his suitcases disappear, but this time he did not despair. His step was eager as he set off towards the royal palace, asking the way of passers-by from time to time.

When he came presently to the distant town, the storm had passed as suddenly as it had broken. Everything seemed washed clean by it. The earth smelt fresh, the rain had touched off a hundred different scents. Innumerable frogs croaked a chorus of *co-ash, co-ash* from nearby paddy-fields, bulbuls cried gaily as they fluttered through the peepul trees. Even the smoke of red dust had been subdued for a while. A silvery tinkle of water came from the gutters.

Kishkar knew in his heart what he was going to attempt, though he did not yet dare to admit it, and for the moment

146

he kept his secret hidden in the darkest corner of his mind.

He thought he would have difficulty getting anywhere near the palace, but as he approached the big, rambling, yellow and white building with its carved wooden pillars and bulbous roofs, he found that crowds of townsfolk were hurrying that way. From the talk around him he learnt that the rajah was celebrating some important event, and the people were to be allowed to watch the festivities. Dances had been arranged, and a band could already be heard playing somewhere in the compound.

"They say the English emperor has given our rajah a medal!"

"There are very important guests. Even the Viceroy has come from Delhi in the north!"

"That is not so. It is the Governor from such-and-such a state. I saw him myself, escorted by lancers. . . ."

Kishkar's interest in the gossip ceased as he jostled with the crowd through the main gates of the palace compound. Furtively, cautiously, keeping an eye on the patrolling chowkidars who twirled their lathis threateningly, he detached himself from the throng and surveyed the various buildings on the other side of the darkening compound.

He must find the tourist, but how difficult it would be— he might be anywhere in that huge palace. Before Kishkar could so much as set foot on the broad steps he would be pounced upon and thrown out.

Now the palace was pricked with innumerable lights. Brocaded chairs were being set in position on the steps, and dancers in elaborate costumes and fearsome masks were assembling at one side. The crowd was allowed to advance as far as a rope that was stretched across the compound, where the people stood chattering in excitement as they waited impatiently for the rajah and his court to appear.

Racked with fear and anxiety, Kishkar wandered away round the side of the palace, which faced a smaller building that was evidently a guest-house. He was afraid because he might be caught, anxious because he might be able to do nothing. Unless he could discover where the tourist and his wife were staying in the palace he was helpless.

Then, as he stood hesitantly between the palace and the guest-house, but listening intently above the sound of the band for approaching footsteps, he saw more lights go on in the guest-house. Someone emerged on to the balcony and stood gazing down into the grounds.

It was a white sahib. It was the tourist.

Kishkar drew back into the shadows. His mouth was dry, his heart beat wildly. Tomkins Sahib was smoking. Kishkar could see the glow of red at the end of a huge cigar, could smell the pungent tobacco.

"Do hurry up, Dolly!" Tomkins called irritably over his shoulder. "We're late already. We mustn't keep H.H. waiting."

"I'm almost ready!" the mem-sahib replied from inside a bedroom. "Just come and fasten my necklace for me...."

Kishkar crouched behind a hedge of bougainvillea. He shivered as he waited and the bougainvillea rustled in response. His breath came in a shuddering sigh and the muscles of his thighs trembled with tension. Now turbanned courtiers appeared from the palace to escort the Honourable Tomkins and his mem-sahib to the entertainment.

Kishkar was certain somebody would hear or see him, but they were all talking loudly as they passed. Tomkins Sahib was wearing a white jacket and black trousers. His mem-sahib rustled as she walked and something glittered in her hair. She smelt strongly, like many strange flowers.

The band clashed and trumpeted from the front of the palace. The crowd murmured reverently as the rajah and his guests took up their places. As if he were a spectator, Kishkar made his way to the edge of the crowd. He must first of all be quite certain that the tourist and his wife were safely seated on the steps before he attempted what he had come to do.

Now the band had stopped playing. The group of dancers filed through a gap in the crowd, leering from their grotesque masks. Musicians squatted at the foot of the steps, slapping on long, cylindrical drums with the palms of their hands. Now certain of the dancers were seating themselves round a large, wide-mouthed copper vessel which a man was beating to give them the time for the high-pitched songs they began to sing. The drummer steadily beat more rapidly, the singing grew more and more intense and one of the actors started to fling himself round in a weird, frenetic dance, while the bangles on his wrists and ankles jingled in accompaniment. The audience watched wide-eyed as the dancer whirled round in a growing frenzy. In one of the brocaded chairs on the palace steps Tomkins Sahib sat with legs crossed, puffing at his cigar.

Kishkar silently withdrew, unremarked by anyone, for the jostling, gaping crowd was too absorbed in the contortions of the perspiring, painted dancer, whose performance was rising to a nerve-racking climax.

Now Kishkar exultingly let his secret have full rein— he was going to retrieve the sacred Buffalo Bell that the white man had violated the dairy-temple to obtain, so that the life of the People of the Buffalo would be restored to health. The storm that had disturbed the peace of the Blue Hills would subside. He was no longer afraid.

Kishkar did not know exactly where he would find the Buffalo Bell, but he thought that it must be in one of those shining leather cases belong to the white man. Somewhere in the guest-house he would find it.

In the hallway of the wooden house he listened intently. Chik-chak lizards called as they performed their acrobatics, crickets chirped shrilly, the timbers of the house relaxed.

Tensely Kishkar began to mount the wooden staircase. He knew that the white sahib and his mem-sahib had been in an upstairs room and guessed they might have their luggage there. It was a strange place . . . Kishkar had never been in such a house before.

The lights from the palace faintly lit up the guest-house and Kishkar could find his way quite well in those un-accustomed surroundings. But as he reached the landing another light flooded the stairs. With a breath of dismay he turned to look.

At the foot of the stairs stood a bearded, turbanned chowkidar, a torch in one hand, a cane lathi in the other.

"Thief!" shouted the chowkidar at the top of his voice and, running to the door of the guest-house, "Thief!" he yelled again. Then he came bounding up the staircase after Kishkar.

17 *Accuser and Accused*

KISHKAR quailed when he beheld the rajah, fatter than
ever at close quarters. He remembered thinking he would
not like to fall into the rajah's hands—that man at the hunt
had screamed horribly when he was beaten. And now,
held securely by two chowkidars, Kishkar faced the rajah
across the room, whose scintillating brilliance he saw only
as a blur of colour.

After they had caught him, the chowkidars had guarded
him in the palace stables, where the palace syces and the
sweepers and water-carriers had gathered to stare at the
thief. They had beaten him and cuffed him, twisted his
arms and stamped on his toes. They had called him a
variety of evil names in a variety of languages, just to make
certain he understood.

When the entertainment was over and the rajah, with his
guests and courtiers, had returned to the throne-room in
the palace, two chowkidars were ordered to bring Kishkar
before him. Ordinarily the rajah would not have bothered
with such a matter: he would have left it until another
day, or had the thief handed over to an English magistrate.
But he was furious that his guests should be robbed and
was determined to show the Honourable Tomkins Sahib
how sternly he meted out justice.

The rajah sat on a gaddi, a cross between a throne and a
bed, leaning against a bolster, with a servant behind him,

waving a peacock fan. Round him stood clustered his sirdars and courtiers, while Tomkins Sahib and his memsahib and Baring Sahib sat near by on brocaded chairs, looking suitably magisterial.

"Now tell us exactly what this thief did," the rajah ordered, and the first chowkidar proceeded to render an elaborate account of what had happened. It lacked nothing in the telling. He was clearly intent on making his master realize what an astute fellow he was.

"But had it not been for my keen perception, lord," the second chowkidar interposed presently, "this hill-boy—as I perceive him to be—would have escaped with all that he had stolen."

"I stole nothing," Kishkar protested sullenly.

"That was only because you were caught," said the rajah quickly, glancing knowingly at Tomkins Sahib.

"I did not come to steal, sahib," Kishkar answered quietly. All the eyes in the room were staring at him and it felt as if every one of them was a dart. He had never in his life been confronted by so many eminent personages, all richly garbed, and he was overawed by them.

"You lost your way, then, I suppose?" the rajah asked sarcastically from among his many chins.

"No, sahib. I came to claim my property—or the property of my people."

"What cock and bull story is this? Tell the truth and it will be better for you."

"I am telling the truth, sahib. I came to look for the sacred bell. . . ."

"The bell? A bell? The boy is mad or feigns madness!"

A tittering laugh rippled among the assembled sirdars, and the chowkidars shook Kishkar reproachfully. The rajah bent over and explained in English for Tomkins's benefit. Tomkins Sahib frowned slightly as he surveyed Kishkar, though it was clear Kishkar meant nothing to him. One black or brown face was the same as any other to Tomkins Sahib.

"The white sahib came to the Blue Hills and stole the sacred Buffalo Bell of my people," Kishkar began to explain, wincing under the grip of the two bearded watchmen who towered over him. He got no further.

With a cry of rage, the rajah sat upright on the gaddi. Instinctively his sirdars flinched back in the face of his anger. The servant with the peacock fan stopped fanning for a moment and then hurriedly resumed his task.

"Do not add lies to your thieving!" the rajah screamed, and all his chins shook in unison. "It is bad enough to come slimily stealing, like a serpent crawling up a drain-pipe, but it is a thousand times worse to insult my guests!"

"But, sahib . . ."

"I will hear no more. Take him away and beat him as if you were threshing grain!"

As the chowkidars began to drag Kishkar away, the sirdars alongside the rajah parted to allow someone to come through. It was the young prince who had led the hunt. At his side padded Hansia the cheetah. She limped slightly but seemed otherwise none the worse for her mishap. Her neat small head was held proudly as she surveyed the assembled company with her tawny eyes. Tame and confident as a hunting-dog, she walked close against her master.

The prince saluted his father by brushing a hand across forehead, heart and lips, and bowed to the white guests in turn. Then he sat down in a vacant chair at the foot of the gaddi, watching idly as the chowkidars manhandled Kishkar towards the main doors.

153

Hansia, too, lay down in front of the prince. But suddenly her head went up alertly, her muzzle wavered questioningly. She sprang up and went padding down the room after Kishkar and his captors.

The whole assembly murmured in surprise, even Baring Sahib raised his eyebrows. The two watchmen were alarmed when they realized what was happening. They let go of Kishkar's arms and stood foolishly to one side, at a loss to know what to do.

Kishkar smiled, he was not afraid. He felt now that he had a friend in this place. He held out a hand and Hansia trotted towards him. He fondled her head as she rubbed herself eagerly against him, her purring loud in the sudden silence.

Everyone stared in utter astonishment; clearly there was something extraordinary here.

The young prince stood up, a frown of mingled disapproval and astonishment on his face. He spoke urgently to his father, questioning him about Kishkar. It was imperative to find out the explanation of Hansia's behaviour. The prince was jealous that his cheetah should be friendly to any but himself.

"Bring that boy back!" the rajah ordered, irritably. The matter had gone on too long and the rajah was hungry.

This time the chowkidars did not seize Kishkar by the arms, but discreetly brought up the rear as he approached the rajah, with Hansia walking by his side.

"Why does my cheetah befriend you like this?" demanded the prince. "Have you some magic influence over animals?"

"No, sahib," Kishkar answered respectfully. "She befriends me now because I once befriended her."

"How so? What riddle is this?"

"When you went hunting, sahib, the cheetah was caught in a trap. . . ."

"He is making it up," the rajah muttered, lolling against the bolster. "He sees her limp and guesses the rest."

"She has a scar on the inner thigh of her right hind leg," Kishkar said, in proof of his story.

"This is all true," the prince declared, leaning forward intently. "This boy does not lie. What were you doing that you were able to heal my Hansia?"

So Kishkar recounted everything that had happened. He told the prince of the People of the Buffalo, of how the white tourist had stolen the sacred Buffalo Bell, and of the trouble that had befallen as a result. He explained how precious Moon Horn was to him and why he and his brother had fled from the Blue Hills with her. He described his encounter with the villagers, and then how he had crossed the river and escaped from the crocodile. He told how he had met the Jangama, whose medicine had helped to heal the wound in Hansia's leg. He even admitted how, for the sake of Tipane and the Jangama, he had stolen from the rajah's picnic.

"For that I am truly sorry, sahib," he finished. "But we were very hungry."

The prince's face was brooding with anger, but it was not anger against Kishkar. He spoke at length in an undertone to his father and the rajah became more and more uncomfortable as he listened to his son. From time to time he eyed Tomkins Sahib who was beginning to look less composed than usual.

At last the prince left his father and stood up again. He bowed coldly to the Honourable Tomkins and spoke to him in English.

"This boy accuses you of stealing a sacred bell from the

temple of his people," the prince said. "Is this true, Tomkins Sahib?"

"I? Steal?" Tomkins Sahib blustered, glancing round at Baring as if for support. "A bell? What on earth. . . ?"

"It was in the Blue Hills, Horace," Mem-sahib Tomkins laid a hand on her husband's arm. "A week or two ago. . . ."

"Oh, that!" Tomkins Sahib nodded slowly, as if it were all just coming back to him. "Those odd people who kept buffaloes. I didn't think it mattered much, you know. Just a souvenir. I try to pick up something wherever I go. You know, masks, carvings, weapons, that sort of thing. . . ."

His voice trailed off as he avoided the prince's eye.

"It was not a good thing to violate the temple of this boy's people," said the prince. In his jewelled turban, embroidered coat and muslin jodhpurs he looked very tall and commanding as he stood near the Honourable Tomkins, who sat deflated in his chair. "My father and I are Moslems, yet most of our subjects are Hindus. Some are pagans, with gods of their own, a few are Christians, like yourself. But we do not interfere with any. All people are entitled to their beliefs provided they do not harm others. The beliefs of all people deserve to be respected."

"It was a silly thing to do," muttered Tomkins Sahib, wiping his forehead with a silk handkerchief, for it suddenly seemed awfully hot in the crowded room. "The boy shall have his bell back; now."

18 *The Storm Passes*

WRAPPED in his stately cloak, Paramajoti the dairy-priest stood with hands clasped under the thicket of his beard, leaning on his staff. Earnestly he gazed out across the undulating ranges of the Blue Hills that were lapped in a milk-white mist tranquil as some strange, magic sea. Already the placid mist was tinted with gold that seemed to pour over the highest range from the rising sun.

It was that moment of undisturbed silence when the hunters and hunted of the night-side had departed to their lairs and the people and creatures of daylight had not yet fully stirred. For twelve mornings now Paramajoti had come to the hill to contemplate. Ever since disaster had shattered the calm life of the People of the Buffalo he had come here in the hope of being vouchsafed some sign from the gods.

He had cleansed and sanctified the temple after its violation, he had recited holy mantras until his voice was hoarse, he had washed the idols with water brought from the holy river in the valley, he had made all the people wash themselves in the same holy river. When that was done they had brought many offerings to the temple, particularly of lamps, and the temple and precincts had burned and twinkled for many days and nights with the flames from them.

All this and much more Paramajoti had done or caused

to be done. Particularly powerful was the special puja he had carried out in secret, witnessed by no other man it was so solemn a worship. . . .

All this was necessary, for Paramajoti knew, even more than the people themselves, that a grievous harm had been done. It was as if a terrible sickness had been spread, leaving the people listless and feeble in body and spirit. The sacred Buffalo Bell might seem a trifling souvenir to others, but to the People of the Buffalo it was the well-spring of their way of life. Paramajoti was full of fore-boding. He knew that the people looked to him for guid-ance and assurance. Yet he felt helpless to avert the ill that pressed down upon them.

That was why he was here now on the hill. He knew that the gods would never return to the dairy-temple now that the Buffalo Bell had been stolen. Only here on the lonely hill was there the least possibility that he might be able to commune with them and learn their wishes. Once again he gazed in fervent hope as the earth was reborn in the miracle of the sunrise. Forlornly the old man kept his vigil and his eyes ached wearily as he watched the hills.

Faintly a bell rang in his head. His thoughts were always so concentrated on the sacred bell that he began to imagine he could hear it, tolling, tolling, in the distance of his brain. He grunted despondently, and rubbed his eyes.

Now the fiery rim of the sun was surging like a chariot above the sweep of the hills. The sea of mist was on fire, branch and leaf were gilded in a transparent glory. In the coombs, among the blue-gum trees, birds were plung-ing and screeching, uttering their praise of another day.

The old man turned, shoulders bowed. The gods were still silent in their displeasure. Irritably he clapped a hand to his ear to drive away the persistent tolling.

Then he frowned and listened intently. Was it imagination or could he really hear a bell, coming and going, far away? Rapidly, with renewed vigour, he hurried across the downs to a gorse-covered knoll from which he could look down into one of the coombs.

Above the mounting thrum of insects and the strident chatter of birds, he tried to concentrate on that elusive sound. But as he stood there, clasping his staff so hard that his fingernails gouged his hand, he knew that the sound was no trick of the imagination.

Faint, far away, spasmodic, it was truly the clanging of a bell. But it was more than that. Paramajoti knew it was the Buffalo Bell itself. No other bell had the same sonorous tone. The gods had relented. The People of the Buffalo would be restored to health and dignity.

Joyfully the old priest hobbled across the dew-soaked turf towards the village, where the smoke of cooking-fires was beginning to curl sulkily above the tunnel-huts. People crawled out through the tiny stoop-doorways as they heard the urgent summons of the priest. At first they feared that Paramajoti had taken leave of his senses, he was so incoherent. But then they too heard the bell, coming and going, still faint far down in the valley, but growing louder all the time.

Led by the dairy-priest, the people started eagerly down the hill in the direction of the sound. They began to run ahead, while Paramajoti laboured on in the rear. Nobody ran faster than Laxam and Sadamut, for the two girls knew that the tolling of the Buffalo Bell could only mean that Kishkar and Tipane were returning.

When Kishkar was reunited with his brother, he had hung the sacred bell round Moon Horn's neck. Then there had still been many miles for the coppersmith bird to record before they reached the Blue Hills again, but there was no weariness in their feet now. Gladly they climbed the road that wound upwards to the Blue Hills. Their feet tingled when for the first time they touched again the resilient turf.

Their pace quickened as they heard the welcoming cries of the people, who came thronging down to meet them. Kwodron and Moutouvelli, Teipakh, Punog, mighty Kunparadi, none had remained behind. Even Kushken shared in the exultation, and Paramajoti still hobbled on, shouting benedictions.

Ahead of them all Laxam and Sadamut ran, first, even though they had paused to gather flowers on the way, plucking fronds of jasmine from wild brakes along the track. Breathless, happy almost to the point of tears, they greeted the two brothers.

Kishkar and Tipane smiled shyly but triumphantly as the girls placed garlands round their necks. Then Moon Horn, too, was garlanded with flowers, and the Buffalo Bell tolled lightly as the heifer stretched out her damp muzzle to snuff the fragrance of the Blue Hills.